THE DREAM
OF HEROES

Adolfo Bioy Casares

THE DREAM OF HEROES

Translated from the Spanish by Diana Thorold

E. P. DUTTON   NEW YORK

First published in the United States in 1988 by E. P. Dutton, a division of NAL Penguin Inc., 2 Park Avenue, New York, N.Y. 10016.

Published simultaneously in Canada by Fitzhenry and Whiteside, Limited, Toronto.

Originally published in Argentina in 1954 under the title El Sueño de los Héroes.

Original English-language publication in 1987 by Quartet Books, Limited, London.

Library of Congress Cataloging-in-Publication Data

Bioy Casares, Adolfo.
The dream of heroes.

Translation of: El sueño de los héroes.
I. Title.
PQ7797.B535S913 1988   863   88-20196

ISBN: 0-525-24687-8

1 3 5 7 9 10 8 6 4 2

First American Edition

Translator's Acknowledgements

First I should like to give special thanks to Adolfo Bioy Casares for his assistance and unfailing encouragement from the start of this project. For the help they have given me in trying to meet the many challenges this book presents for the translator, I also want to express my warmest thanks to Robert Chandler, John King, Ian Sutton and Celia Szusterman, and above all to Emily Lane and Juan Masoliver.

Translator's Preface

Adolfo Bioy Casares has always shown an interest in combining the real and the fantastic. His acclaimed earlier works such as *The Invention of Morel* (1940; University of Texas, 1985) and *A Plan for Escape* (1945; Graywolf, 1988) are intense, elliptical and abstract, but while the intensity is still present in later works, there is also a relaxed quality, with the metaphysical speculations solidly grounded in a social and cultural context. *The Dream of Heroes* (1954) is the supreme example of this union. The novel gives a real sense of lived experience, of a concrete time and place – the suburbs of Buenos Aires in the late 1920s – and throughout Bioy displays his masterly ear for dialogue. At the same time the story moves effortlessly beyond realism into the mysterious and the magical. As well as the incidents of everyday life it is clear that something else is going on; another dimension is present.

The book is among other things a meditation on the nature of courage and the macho ideal. That Buenos Aires of the 1920s, which was mythologized by Borges in his writing of the time, such as *El Sur* – key elements being men of courage, the knife-fighter, the *barrio* or neighbourhood, the tango – is here given a documentary solidity. The cult of courage, honour and violence that had originated with the gauchos is seen to be debased once it is transferred to the city, though the appeal to courage still retains immense power. The observation, detail and dark humour of these episodes concerning the boys and the sinister Valerga, their 'leader', are among the most striking features of the book, which is the story of the hero Emilio Gauna's quest and its eventual resolution, on the third day of the Carnival of 1930.

The story is told with a fine economy of means yet with perfect clarity, the stages of realization in the reader's mind keeping pace with the stages of discovery in Gauna's. Many of the ingredients of classic quest literature, such as a long journey with an unknown destination, a series of tests, helpers with special knowledge and magical powers, are present in a veiled or parodied form. When we reach the climax of the story it seems unexpected yet inevitable. The resolution is deliberately sought and at the same time ordained. Gauna consciously wills his own destiny: in reconstructing the events of the Carnival three years earlier he seems to be forcing what was a premonition to come true. The distinction between free will and predestination disappears.

The events of the third day of the Carnival of 1927 had introduced Gauna (though he was unaware of it) to a world of values very different from that of Valerga and his corrupt heroism. This is represented by the 'Sorcerer' Taboada and his daughter Clara. Gauna's love for Clara begins as an attempt to win prestige among his friends but deepens into real tenderness as well as passion. Of Clara's father, who claims clairvoyant gifts, he is at first contemptuous, but he learns to value and admire him. Taboada's powers are, in fact, deep and inexplicable. Underneath the novel's surface realism it is not fanciful to read it as the struggle for Gauna's soul, with two alternative father figures for the orphaned boy – Taboada (despite the author's occasional affectionate mockery of him) standing for Good, and Valerga for Evil. There is an undoubted reference in this struggle between 'civilization and barbarism' to a whole tradition of Argentine writing which goes back to the mid nineteenth century. The interior conflict in Gauna is symbolized in the 'magical' duel, and Gauna's quest for self-discovery brings out all Bioy's subtle and ironic art.

The Dream of Heroes can thus be read on many levels and not all its meanings reveal themselves straight away.

It is social comment and moral allegory; it is a love story and a thriller; a mystery and a technical *tour-de-force*. The style modulates skilfully in keeping with the mood and environment of the different episodes; and there is also a great deal of exuberant humour. In the course of the novel Bioy sheds light on a whole range of human experience: on man's understanding (or misunderstanding) of woman, on the nature of true courage and the macho myth, on the impossibility of separating reality from imagination. With all its intriguing strangeness, this is a world which everyone will recognize.

THE DREAM
OF HEROES

I

During the three days and nights of the carnival of 1927
the life of Emilio Gauna reached its first mysterious
climax. It is difficult to decide whether someone had
foreseen the terrible end decreed and had altered the
chain of events from afar. Of course to claim that an
obscure demiurge was responsible for events which our
poor human intelligence in its haste vaguely attributes to
destiny, would add a new problem without shedding new
light. What Gauna glimpsed towards the end of the third
night became for him like a magic possession he longed to
regain, won and lost in a marvellous adventure. In the
years immediately following he became obsessed with
trying to investigate and recall that experience. This
constant topic of conversation greatly discredited him in
the eyes of his friends.

These friends met every night in the Platense Club, on
the corner of Iberá and avenida Del Tejar, and when Dr
Valerga, mentor and model for them all, was not with
them, they talked about football. Sebastián Valerga was a
man of few words and prone to hoarseness. He talked
about the turf – the palpitating contests of bygone days
– politics and courage. Gauna would occasionally have
liked to talk about Hudsons and Studebakers, Rafaela's
five-hundred-mile race or Córdoba's Audax, but as the
others were not interested he had to keep quiet. This gave
him a sort of inner life. On Saturdays or Sundays they
went to watch their team, Platense, play. Some Sundays,
if they had time, they stopped in at the stuccoed café

called the Argonauts – to laugh at the girls, they said.

Gauna was just twenty-one, slim and narrow-shouldered, with dark curly hair and greenish eyes. He had arrived in the neighbourhood two or three months before. His family was from the town of Tapalqué; he remembered its dusty streets and the morning light when he took his dog Gabriel for walks. Orphaned when very young, he had been taken by some relations to Villa Urquiza. There he had got to know Larsen, a boy his own age, a bit taller and red-haired. Some years later Larsen moved to Saavedra. Gauna had always wanted to earn his own living and not be indebted to anyone. When Larsen got him a job in Lambruschini's garage, Gauna moved to Saavedra too and rented a room with his friend two blocks from the park.

Larsen had introduced him to the boys and to Dr Valerga. The meeting with Valerga made a deep impression on him. The Doctor embodied one of the ways in which Gauna had always dreamed of his life developing, without seriously considering it possible. We will not yet speak of the influence this admiration had on Gauna's destiny.

One Saturday Gauna was being shaved at the barber's shop in calle Conde. The barber, Massantonio, mentioned a colt which was running that afternoon at Palermo. It was sure to win and would pay out at more than 50 to 1. Not to put a really fat bet on it would be idiotic: a lost opportunity short-sighted misers who can't see past their own noses would live to regret. Massantonio was so tedious and insistent that Gauna, who had never bet on a horse in his life, gave him the thirty-six pesos he had on him. He then asked for a pencil and took down the colt's name on the back of a tram ticket: Meteoric.

That same evening at a quarter to eight Gauna went into the Platense Club with the *Ultima Hora* under his arm and said to the boys:

'Thanks to Massantonio the barber, I've won 1,000 pesos on the races. Let's spend it together.'

He spread the paper open on the table and read laboriously:

2

'Sixth race at Palermo – winner Meteoric. Odds – 59.30 to 1.'

Pegoraro did not hide his resentment and incredulity. He was fat, heavy-featured, cheerful, impulsive, noisy and – a secret everyone shared – had boils all over his legs. Gauna looked at him for a moment, then took out his wallet and half-opened it to show the wad of notes. Antúnez, who was called 'El Largo Barolo' or 'El Pasaje',* because of his size, remarked:

'That's too much for one night's drinking.'

'The carnival goes on for more than one night,' declared Gauna.

A boy who looked like a dummy in a local shop-window interrupted. He was called Maidana and nicknamed 'El Gomina', Brilliantine. He advised Gauna to set up on his own. He remembered there was a newspaper stall up for sale at a railway station. He added: 'Tolosa or Tristán Suárez. I can't remember which. Quite near but pretty dead.'

Pegoraro thought Gauna should rent an office in the smart northern part of town and open an employment agency.

'You can loll back behind a desk with your private telephone. New arrivals to the city come trooping in and you get five pesos out of each of them.'

Antúnez suggested he give him all the money. He'd hand it over to his father and within a month Gauna would get back four times the amount.

'The law of compound interest,' he added.

'There'll be plenty of time later to save and scrape,' replied Gauna. 'This time we're all going to enjoy ourselves.'

Larsen backed him up. Then Antúnez proposed:

'Let's ask the Doctor.'

No one dared contradict him. Gauna paid for another round of vermouth, they drank to better times, and set off

---

*A local reference. El Pasaje Barolo, the Barolo Building, was for many years the highest in Buenos Aires and is one of the few arcades.

for Dr Valerga's house. When they were in the street, in that fine vibrato voice that was to win him a certain fame years later at fairs and charity performances, Antúnez began singing *La Copa del Olvido*. Gauna, in a spirit of friendly envy, reflected that Antúnez always found the right tango for the occasion.

It had been a hot day and people were sitting chatting in groups in their doorways. Truly inspired, Antúnez sang at the top of his voice. Gauna had the strange impression of watching himself go by with the boys amidst the disapproval and resentment of the neighbours and felt a certain joy and a certain pride in this. He looked at the trees, their foliage motionless against the purplish evening sky. Larsen gave the singer a slight nudge. He stopped singing. They were barely fifty metres from Dr Valerga's house.

As usual the Doctor opened the door himself. He was a stout man, with a large, well-shaven, bronzed but singularly inexpressive face. However, when he laughed – dropping his jaw and revealing his upper teeth and tongue – he had an expression of gentle, almost effeminate softness. Between his shoulders and his waist, his body, which bulged slightly around the stomach, was extraordinarily long. He moved with a certain heaviness, full of force, as though pushing something. He let them in one by one, examining their faces carefully. This amazed Gauna, because there was quite enough light and the Doctor must have known immediately who they were.

It was a low house. The Doctor took them down a side passage through a room that had been a patio into his study, which had two balconies overlooking the street. On the walls there were a number of photographs of people eating in restaurants or under trellises or around barbecues, and two solemn portraits: one of Dr Luna, vice-president of the Republic, and the other of Dr Valerga himself. The house gave an impression of tidiness, poverty and a certain dignity. With almost exaggerated politeness the Doctor asked them to sit down.

'To what do I owe this honour?' he asked.

Gauna did not reply at once because he thought he discerned in the tone a veiled and to him a mysterious hint

4

of sarcasm. Larsen stammered out something quickly but the Doctor went out. Gauna asked:

'Who's that woman?'

He could see her beyond the room, on the other side of the patio. Draped in black, she was sitting in a very low chair, sewing. She was old.

Gauna thought no one had heard him. A moment later Maidana replied as if waking up:

'She's the Doctor's servant.'

Dr Valerga came back in with three bottles of beer and some glasses on a little tray. He put them down on the desk and served his guests. One of them wanted to talk but the Doctor would not let him. For a moment he made them feel ill at ease, protesting that it was an important gathering and that only the person duly appointed should speak. They all looked at Gauna, who finally plucked up the courage to say:

'I've won 1,000 pesos on the races and I think the best way of spending it is for all of us to go and enjoy ourselves at the carnival.'

The Doctor looked at him without expression. Gauna thought, 'I've been too impetuous – I've offended him.' Nevertheless he added:

'I hope you'll honour us with your company.'

'I don't work in a circus – I haven't got a company,' replied the Doctor smiling. Then he added seriously: 'I think that's a very good idea, my friend. One should always be generous with money won by betting.'

The tension eased. They all went into the kitchen and came back with a plate of cold meat and more bottles of beer. After eating and drinking they got the Doctor to tell stories. The Doctor took a little mother-of-pearl penknife out of his pocket and began cleaning his nails.

'Talking of gambling,' he said, 'I remember an evening around 1921, when Maneglia invited me to his office. You remember him, don't you – enormously fat, shook like a jelly? But when he handled cards his touch was as light as a lady's. I don't reckon I'm an envious sort of person' – he glanced sharply at each of the others – 'but I always envied him for that. And I'm still amazed even now at

5

what the late lamented Maneglia could do with his hands, before you knew what was happening. Still, it didn't do him any good. One morning he got drenched with the dew, and within twenty-four hours he had died of double pneumonia.

'That evening we'd had dinner together, and he asked me to go back with him to his office, where some of his friends were waiting for him to play *truco*.* I didn't know that he had an office, or even a job, but as it was oppressively hot, and we'd had quite a lot to eat, I thought I would like to get a breath of air before going to bed. I was surprised that he agreed to walk with me, especially when I saw how quickly he got out of breath. I hadn't yet realized how mean he was, and how obsessed with money. But I was most surprised of all when he turned in at the entrance to an undertaker's. He stopped, and without looking at me said: "Here we are. Won't you come in?" I have always had a revulsion about anything to do with death, so I had to force myself, very reluctantly, to walk between two rows of hearses and go in. We climbed a spiral staircase and his office was at the top. His friends were waiting for him there, in a haze of smoke. I can't pretend to remember exactly what they looked like. Or rather I know there were two of them, and the face of one was very badly burnt – one big scar, if you see what I mean. They told Maneglia that a third man – they mentioned his name, but I didn't pay attention – couldn't come. Maneglia didn't seem surprised, and asked me to stand in for the missing man. Without waiting for my answer he opened a wooden cupboard, took out the cards and put them on the table. Then he fetched some bread and two yellow *dulce de leche*‡ jars. One contained beans for us to use as counters; the other contained dulce de leche. We cut for partners, but I realized already that this was a mere formality. Whoever was my partner would be Maneglia's partner too.

'At first our luck was about equal. When the phone

---

*A kind of poker.

‡A thick jam made of milk and sugar, cheap and popular.

6

rang, he would take his time in answering it – "I don't want to speak with my mouth full," he explained. The amount of bread and dulce de leche he could eat was phenomenal. After putting the phone down, he would get up heavily, open a little window that gave on to the stables, and shout out to the men: "One altar complete with fittings" or "one forty-peso coffin". Then he called out the street name and number. Most of the coffins cost forty pesos. Really powerful whiffs of hay and ammonia, I recall, came through the window.

'I can tell you, I learnt a good deal about sleight-of-hand that evening. Around midnight I really began losing heavily. I realized that the signs were not propitious, as the peasants say, and that I had to do something about it. The whole funereal place was getting me down. Maneglia had pulled so many fast ones, without my being able to make the least protest, that I was fed up. The cheats were beating me again, when Maneglia turned his cards over – an ace, a four and a five – and shouted "Tierce of spades!" "Tierce of cuts!" I replied, and picking up an ace I drew the side of the card across his face. The great fat man began bleeding like an ox. The blood went everywhere. Even the bread and the dulce were red with it. Slowly I gathered up all the money on the table and put it in my pocket. Then I picked up a handful of cards and mopped up the blood, and wiped it all over his snout. Finally I walked calmly out of the room and no one tried to stop me. Some time afterwards, the late lamented Maneglia slandered me to mutual friends, saying I had a knife under the card. The poor man thought everyone was as clever with their fingers as he was.'

II

It is not true that the boys had doubted Dr Valerga, even once. They understood that things were now different. When the time came, Dr Valerga would not fail them. One might ask, a trifle sarcastically, why, in that case, they seemed to put off that 'time', and even did what they could to stop it coming. Perhaps they were afraid of being themselves cast in the role of victims in some sudden act of violence. Perhaps Larsen and Gauna, in the course of a confidential talk that neither of them ever referred to again, told each other that the Doctor's fondness for stories of which he was the hero should not be held against him. If you were a brave man these days there was little you could do but recount past exploits. If someone were to ask why this man who spent so much of his time talking about himself had the reputation of being taciturn and reserved, we would reply that perhaps it was all a question not of what is said but *how* it is said, the voice and the tone. Think of some of the ironic men you have known. Would you not agree that irony in the lips, the eyes and the voice is much more effective than irony just in the words?

For Gauna there had been allusions and secret reverberations in that conversation about Dr Valerga's courage. 'Larsen,' he thought, 'no doubt remembers the time when I crossed the street to avoid fighting the washerwoman's son. Or the time when that little frog Vaisman – he really did look like a frog – came to the house with Fernandito Fonseca. I must have been six or seven; I had only just come to Villa Urquiza. I had a sort of admiration for Fernandito and a certain affection for Vaisman. Vaisman came into the house alone. He said Fernandito had told him I had been saying nasty things about him and he had come to fight me. I let myself get very upset by the betrayal and Fernandito's lies, and I refused to fight. As he was leaving I saw Fernandito leering at me from behind a tree. A few days later Larsen met him on open ground; they talked about me, and a little while after that the boys saw Fernandito hanging onto a woman's hand: he was limping, his nose was bleeding, and he was crying...

'Maybe Larsen remembers my seventh birthday too. Full of a sense of importance at being seven, I agreed to a boxing match with a bigger boy. He didn't want to hurt me and the fight went on and on. It was going fine until I lost my patience. Maybe I began wondering how it could ever end. Anyway, at that point I lay down on the ground and burst into tears ... And perhaps he remembers the Sunday when I had a fight with that boy Martelli. He was a mulatto, freckled, and with very solid hips and thighs. As I was beating a tattoo on his midriff for all I was worth he asked me how I could possibly hit so hard. For a second or two I thought he was serious. Then I noticed that on his lips, blue outside and pink as raw meat inside, there was a repulsive smile.'

What Larsen in fact remembered was a certain afternoon when a rabid dog had suddenly appeared and Gauna had kept it off with a stick until he and the other boys could get away. He also remembered a night he had spent at Gauna's house. There were just the two of them and Gauna's aunt. Shortly before dawn burglars broke in. He and the aunt were paralysed with fear, but Gauna had made a noise with a chair and said, 'Here's the revolver, uncle,' as if his uncle were there. Then he calmly went outside and looked round the courtyard. Larsen, from the back of the bedroom, saw the glow of the lantern shining up at the sky above the wall and saw Gauna below, unarmed, tiny, bony: the very image of bravery.

Larsen thought he knew that Gauna was brave. Gauna

9

thought Larsen was rather timid in everyday life, but would stand up to anybody if the occasion demanded. As for himself he reckoned that he could throw away his life with perfect indifference; if someone had suggested staking it on a throw of dice he would have felt few doubts or fears as he shook the dicebox. But he was repelled by the idea of fighting with his fists. Perhaps he was afraid that he could not hit hard enough and would be laughed at. Or perhaps – this was the explanation later put to him by the Sorcerer Taboada – when he was confronted by a will hostile to his own he just felt an awful weariness and wanted to give in. He thought this was quite a likely explanation, but he feared the true one might be different. At present nobody thought him a weakling. He went around with aspiring toughs and no one saw him as a coward. But it was a fact that almost all their quarrels came to words rather than blows. At football matches there were a few incidents, such as throwing bottles or stones at one another or brawling indiscriminately, in groups. Now, bravery was a matter of keeping your nerve. It was when you were young that you put yourself to the test. For him, the test had shown that he was a coward.

III

That night, after further anecdotes, the Doctor accompanied them to the door.

'Shall we meet here tomorrow at half-past six?' asked Gauna.

'Vermouth will be served at half-past six,' announced Valerga.

The boys walked away in silence. They went into the Platense and ordered rums. Gauna thought aloud: 'I must invite the barber, Massantonio.'

'You should ask the Doctor's opinion first,' said Antúnez.

'We can't go back now,' said Maidana. 'He'll think we're afraid of him.'

'But he'll be annoyed if we don't consult him – that's what I think,' insisted Antúnez.

'Doesn't matter what he thinks,' put in Larsen. 'But imagine his reaction if we go and pester him now, to ask his permission.'

'It's not asking his permission,' said Antúnez.

'Let Gauna go alone,' recommended Pegoraro.

Gauna declared: 'We must invite Massantonio' – he put some coins on the table and got up – 'even if we have to drag him out of bed.'

The prospect of dragging the barber out of bed appealed to them all. Forgetting the Doctor and the scruples they had had about not consulting him, they began wondering what the barber's sleeping arrangements were and they thought up ways of distracting the wife while Gauna talked to the husband. Excited by their schemes, the boys walked quickly and got a bit ahead of Larsen and Gauna. The two of them, as if by agreement, proceeded to pee in the street. Gauna remembered other nights, in other neighbourhoods, when they had also peed together on the asphalt in the light of the moon: he reflected that a friendship like theirs was the most precious thing in a man's life.

The boys were waiting for them in front of the house where the barber lived. Larsen declared with authority: 'Gauna should go in alone.'

As Gauna crossed the first courtyard, a little woolly, yellowish dog, tied to a door-knocker, barked for a moment. He went on, and in the corridor to the left, after the second courtyard, he stopped in front of a door. He knocked, timidly at first, then boldly. The door opened a crack. Massantonio's head appeared; he looked sleepy and slightly balder than usual. 'I've come to invite you,' Gauna began, but he broke off because the barber was blinking so much, 'I've come to invite you,' he spoke slowly and courteously (to someone in a dream or a bit fuddled, it might have seemed as if the young Gauna had turned into the old Valerga), 'to come and help us, the boys and me, spend the 1,000 pesos you made me win on the races.'

The barber still did not understand. Gauna explained: 'Tomorrow at six o'clock we'll be expecting you at Dr Valerga's house and then we'll go and have dinner together.'

The barber was more awake now and listened to him with a distrust he tried to conceal. Gauna did not notice this, and politely and rather tediously pressed the invitation.

'But my wife,' Massantonio begged him, 'I can't leave her.'

'That's just what she'd like, to be left for a while,' replied Gauna, unaware of his rudeness.

He caught a glimpse of blankets and pillows but no sheets on a bed in disorder; he also glimpsed a woman's golden lock and a bare arm.

IV

The next morning Larsen woke up with a sore throat; by the evening he had flu. Gauna had suggested to the boys 'postponing the expedition till a more suitable occasion' but when he saw their disappointment, he dropped the idea. Now, sitting on a little white wooden box, he listened to his friend. Larsen, in his undershirt, wrapped in a blanket and lying on a striped mattress, with his head resting on a very low pillow, began:

'When I flopped into bed last night, I could already feel that I was sickening for something. Today, I felt worse every hour. All morning I was feeling wretched at the thought of not being able to come with you, the thought that by evening my head would be spinning with fever, and by two o'clock it'd happened.'

While he listened to these explanations, Gauna thought fondly of Larsen's character, so different from his own.

'The housekeeper recommends gargling with salt,' said Larsen. 'My mother was always a great believer in gargling with tea. I'd like to hear what you think. But don't imagine I've done nothing; I've already started the campaign with some seaweed. And by the way, if I consulted the Sorcerer Taboada, who knows more than many doctors with diplomas, he would have me throw all these remedies out of the window and spend a week eating so much lemon that the mere thought of it gives me jaundice.'

Talking of flu and of his tactics for combating it almost reconciled Larsen to his destiny, almost put fresh heart into him.

'Be careful you don't catch it,' said Larsen.

'You still believe in all that, do you?'

'Well, it's not a big room. It's a good thing you won't be sleeping here tonight.'

'The boys'll die of disappointment if we don't leave till tomorrow. Not because they particularly want to go, mind you, but because they'd be scared to tell Valerga we'd put it off.'

'Well, that's not surprising.' The tone of Larsen's voice changed. 'Before I forget, how much *did* you win on the races?'

'I've already told you, 1,000 pesos; 1,068 pesos and 30 centavos to be precise. The 68 pesos and 30 centavos are for Massantonio, who gave me the tip.'

Gauna looked at his watch and then added: 'It's time I left. It's a shame you aren't coming.'

'Right, Emilito,' replied Larsen, in an encouraging tone. 'Don't drink too much.'

'If you knew how much I like the stuff, you'd know what strength of will I've got and you wouldn't treat me like a drunkard.'

V

When he saw Massantonio arrive, Dr Valerga did not ask
any questions. Gauna was inwardly grateful for this proof
of tolerance; for his own part he realized it had been a
mistake to invite the barber.

Because they were going out with Valerga, they did not
put on fancy dress. They did not volunteer any opinion on
the subject with the Doctor, but among themselves they
pretended to be way above the whole pantomime and to
look down upon all those dressed in fancy costume.
Valerga wore striped trousers and a dark jacket but unlike
the boys he did not wear a handkerchief round his neck.
Gauna decided that if he had a bit of cash left after the
fiesta he would buy himself some striped trousers too.

Maidana (or maybe it was Pegoraro) suggested they
begin with the Villa Urquiza carnival parade, but Gauna
objected that as he was from that neighbourhood, everyone there would recognize him. No one insisted. Valerga
said they should go to Villa Devoto. 'After all, that's
where we all end up,' he added (a much appreciated
allusion to the prison in that area). In high spirits they set
off for Saavedra station.

The train was full of people in carnival dress. The boys
protested, visibly annoyed. Moved by these complaints,
Valerga played the role of conciliator. The fear that
someone in fancy dress might dare to laugh at the Doctor
or that Massantonio would irritate him with his timidity
scarcely impinged on Gauna's happiness. They passed
through Colegiales and La Paternal and arrived at Villa

15

Devoto (or up at the Villa as Maidana called it) and joined the parade. The Doctor reckoned the carnival was not so lively this year and recounted anecdotes of the carnivals of his youth. They went into the Os Mininos Club and the boys danced. Valerga, the barber (very ill at ease and embarrassed) and Gauna sat at the table and talked. The Doctor spoke of elections and horse-racing. Gauna felt a kind of guilty responsibility towards the Doctor and Massantonio, as well as a slight resentment towards Massantonio.

They went out into the empty plaza Arenales to get some fresh air and then, opposite the Villa Devoto Club, they got caught up in a brief and confused incident with some people who were on the other side of the wire fence.

When the heat had become even more intolerable, a noisy and distinctly disagreeable band of musicians appeared. There were only a few of them but there seemed to be many, with their drums, tambourines and cymbals, their red noses and faces blackened like Negro mamelukes. They shouted hoarsely:

> *And now the band has come,*
> *The young musicians all.*
> *If you buy us each a rum,*
> *We won't perform at all.*

Gauna called a carriage. Despite the protests of the driver and Massantonio's repeated offers to go back home, all seven of them got in. Pegoraro sat on the box next to the driver; Valerga, Massantonio and Gauna sat on the main seat and Antúnez and Maidana on the jump-seats. Valerga ordered the driver: 'To Rivadavia and Villa Luro.' Massantonio tried to jump off. They all wanted to be rid of him but they would not let him leave.

In the course of the journey they met more than one carnival parade, followed them and then lost them; went into shops and other establishments. Massantonio joked in an anguished tone that if he didn't go back at once his wife would beat him to death. At Villa Luro there was an incident with a boy who was lost. Dr Valerga gave him a water squirt – a tube of brilliantine of the Bellas Porteñas

16

brand – and then took him to the police station or to his parents' house. At least that was what Gauna thought he remembered.

It was after three in the morning when they left Villa Luro. They continued by carriage to Flores and then on to Nueva Pompeya. Antúnez was now in the driver's seat; languorously he sang *Noche de Reyes*. Gauna had confused memories of this part of the journey. Someone said that up above Antúnez was busy with something and that the driver was weeping. Gauna had fleeting but vivid images of the horse (which is strange, because he was facing backwards in the carriage). He remembered it as very big and angular, dark with sweat, pawing the air unsteadily, or he heard it crying like a human being (that he had certainly dreamed), or else he saw only its ears and the top of its head and was filled with inexplicable compassion. Afterwards, on a piece of open ground, when the light was a scarcely perceptible lilac at the approach of dawn, there was a feeling of great joy. Gauna himself shouted that they should seize Massantonio, and Antúnez fired his revolver into the air. Finally they arrived on foot at a farm belonging to a friend of the Doctor. Packs of dogs greeted them and then a woman more aggressive than the dogs. The owner was away. The woman did not want to let them come in. Massantonio, talking to himself, explained that he couldn't do without sleep because he had to get up early. Valerga allocated them rooms throughout the house. How they got from there to the next place was a mystery. Gauna remembered waking up in a tin hut; his headache; the journey in a filthy cart and then in a tram; a very bright afternoon and a very bright light in a courtyard at Barracas, where they played bowls; finding out that Massantonio had disappeared, which he heard with surprise and immediately forgot; the night in a brothel in calle Osvaldo Cruz where when he heard a blind violinist playing *Clair de Lune* he felt profound remorse at having neglected his education; an urge to call everyone present his brother; a disdain – loudly proclaimed – for petty selfishness, and an enthusiasm for all noble aspirations. After that he had felt very tired. They had walked through a downpour. To recover, they had gone to a Turkish bath. (Now, however, he saw the downpour falling on the rubbish-tip at Bañado de Flores, and on the dirty sides of the cart.) Of the baths he remembered a kind of manicurist, heavily made up, in a dressing-gown, talking seriously with some unknown man, and an interminable, confused and happy morning. He also remembered going down calle Peru to get away from the police, his legs weak and his mind clear; going into a cinema; being ravenously hungry and having something to eat at five o'clock, among the billiard-tables in a café in avenida de Mayo; taking part in the carnival parades in the centre of town, sitting on the hood of a taxi; going to a performance at the Cosmopolitan, thinking they were at the Bataclán.

They took a second taxi, full of little mirrors and with a devil hanging on a string. Gauna felt very confident when he ordered the driver to go to Palermo, and very proud when he heard Valerga saying, 'You look mere shadows of yourselves, my boys, whereas Gauna and I – old as I am – are still full of energy.' At the door of the Armenonville they bumped into a private car, a Lincoln. Four young boys got out, and a girl who was wearing a mask. If Valerga had not intervened, there would have been a fight between the boys and the taxi-driver; the man did not seem grateful and Valerga reproved him with a few well-chosen words.

Gauna tried to count up the number of times he had been drunk since Sunday afternoon. Never had he had such a headache or felt so tired.

They went into a hall, 'as big as *La Prensa*', explained Gauna, 'or as the hall at Retiro, but without the model train that goes when you put ten centavos in the slot.' It was brightly lit, decorated with streamers, little flags and coloured balls, with poles and draperies, and filled with noisy people and loud music. Gauna held his head tightly in his hands and closed his eyes; he thought he was going to scream with pain. After a while he found himself talking to the girl the boys had brought. She was wearing a mask and a domino cloak. He did not notice whether

18

she was fair or dark but he felt happy beside her (with his headache miraculously relieved), and since that night he had often thought of her.

After a while the boys from the Lincoln came back. When he remembered them he felt that he was dreaming. One of them looked like a national hero from a book of Grosso, with an incredibly thin face. Another was very tall and very pale, as though made of dough; another was fair and also pale, with a big head; another was bow-legged like a jockey. The latter asked him, 'Who do you think you are, stealing our masked girl?', and before he had finished speaking, squared up to him like a boxer. Gauna fingered the little knife in his belt. It was like a dog fight: the two of them very quickly gave it up. At one point Gauna heard Valerga talking in a persuasive and fatherly tone. Then he felt very happy, looked around, and said to his companion, 'We seem to be alone again.' They danced. In the middle of the dance he lost the masked girl. He came back to the table. Valerga and the boys were there. Valerga suggested a walk around the lakes, 'to cool ourselves down a bit so we don't end up in the police station'. He looked up and saw his masked girl with the fair boy at the bar. Depressed and resentful, he agreed to Valerga's suggestion. Antúnez pointed to a bottle of champagne that was already open. They filled their glasses and drank.

After that the memories become distorted and con-fused. The masked girl had disappeared. He asked where she was. They didn't reply, or tried to calm him with evasive replies, as if he were ill. He was not ill. He was tired (at first, lost in the immensity of his exhaustion, heavy and open like the bottom of the sea; finally, in the remote heart of his exhaustion, at peace, almost happy). Then he found himself among trees, surrounded by people, absorbed in the flickering quicksilver reflection of the moon on his knife, inspired, fighting with Valerga because of some quarrel over money. (That was absurd: how could they quarrel over money?)

He opened his eyes. Now the reflection came and went between the floorboards. He guessed that outside, very near perhaps, the morning sun was shining impetuously. He felt a deep, dense pain in his eyes and the nape of his neck. He was in the dark, on a camp-bed, in a room with wooden walls. There was a smell of grass. Below, between the floor-boards – as if the house was upside down and the floor was the roof – he could see the lines of sunlight and a dark sky, green as a bottle. At times the lines widened, a luminous space appeared and there was a swaying movement against the green background. It was water.

A man came in. Gauna asked him where he was.

'Don't you know? On the landing-stage of the lake at Palermo.'

The man brewed him some maté and straightened his pillow in a fatherly way. His name was Santiago. He was around forty, stout, fair-haired and tanned, with kind eyes, a short moustache and a scar on his chin. He had on a blue jersey with long sleeves.

'When I came back last night I found you in the camp-bed. El Mudo was looking after you. Someone brought you here, I suppose?'

'No,' replied Gauna, shaking his head. ' I was found in the wood.'

Shaking his head made him feel sick. He fell asleep again almost immediately. When he woke up he heard a woman's voice. He thought he recognized it. He got up – whether then or much later, he wasn't sure. Every movement set off painful reverberations in his head. In the dazzling light outside, he saw a girl with her back to him. He leant against the door-frame. He wanted to see the girl's face. He wanted to see it because he was sure she was the daughter of the Sorcerer Taboada.

He was mistaken: he did not know her. She must be a washerwoman because she had picked up a flat wicker basket from the ground. Gauna was aware of a kind of hoarse barking noise very near his face. Half-opening his eyes, he turned round. The person who was barking was a man like Santiago but broader in build, darker and clean-shaven. He was wearing a very old grey jersey and blue trousers.

'What do you want?' asked Gauna.

Each word he uttered was like an enormous animal that threatened to split his skull as it moved inside it. The man again began to make awkward guttural sounds. Gauna realized he must be El Mudo. He realized El Mudo wanted him to go back to bed.

He went back indoors and went back to bed. When he woke up he felt somewhat refreshed. Santiago and El Mudo were in the room. He had a friendly conversation with Santiago. They talked about football. Santiago and El Mudo had been caretakers of a club. Gauna spoke about the fifth division at Urquiza, which he had joined straight off the street when he was eleven.

'Once we played against the boys of the KDT club,' said Gauna.

'And the KDT really wiped the floor with you, didn't they?' declared Santiago.

'What do you mean?' replied Gauna. 'We'd already got five goals before they got their only one.'

'El Mudo and I used to work for KDT. We were caretakers.'

'Really? Maybe we met that afternoon.'

'Yes – we must have. I was coming to that. Do you remember the changing-room?'

'How could I forget it? A little wooden building on the left between the tennis courts.'

'Yes, that's it. That's where El Mudo and I lived.'

The possibility that they might have seen each other in those far-off days, confirmed by the discovery of shared memories of the topography of the defunct football club and its little changing-room, helped to ripen their budding friendship.

Gauna spoke of Larsen and of how they had moved to Saavedra.

'Now my team is Platense,' he declared.

'Not a bad team,' replied Santiago. 'But personally, as Aldini used to say, I prefer Excursionistas.'

Santiago went on to explain how they had been left without a job and how they had then got the concession for the lake. Santiago and El Mudo looked like sailors –

two old sea-dogs. Maybe that was because of their job of hiring out boats or maybe because of their jerseys and blue trousers. The two windows of the house were surrounded by life-jackets. There were five pictures hanging on the walls: Umberto Primo; an engaged couple; the Argentine football team that lost against Uruguay in the Olympics; the Excursionistas team (in colour, out of *El Gráfico*); and over El Mudo's camp-bed, El Mudo.

Gauna sat up. 'I'm better now,' he said. 'I think I can go.'

'There's no hurry,' Santiago assured him.

El Mudo brewed some maté. Santiago asked : 'What were you doing in the wood when El Mudo found you?'

'If only I knew,' replied Gauna.

VI

The strangest thing of all is that the core of Gauna's obsession was the adventure of the lakes; the masked girl was for him only a part of that adventure, a very emotive and nostalgic part, but not essential. At least that is what he had communicated, in different words, to Larsen. Perhaps he wanted to play down the importance of anything to do with women. There are signs that could confirm this statement; the snag is that they also contradict it. For example one evening in Palermo he declared: 'In the end it may even turn out that I'm in love.' To speak like this in front of his friends, a man like Gauna must really be blinded by passion. But these words show that he made no attempt to hide it.

Moreover, he himself admitted that he had never seen the girl's face, or that if he had, he had been so drunk that the memory was fantastical and hardly reliable. It is rather curious that this unknown girl should have made so strong an impression on him.

What happened in the wood was also strange. Gauna could never explain it coherently; nor could he forget it. 'If I compare her with that,' he explained, 'she barely matters.' Even so, the image of the girl that remained in his heart was vivid and resplendent, but the splendour came from other visions that he must have had later, when the girl was no longer there.

After the adventure Gauna was never the same. Incredibly enough, this story, confused and vague as it was, gave him a certain prestige among the women, and, according to some, even contributed to the Sorcerer's daughter falling in love with him. All this – the ridiculous change that had taken place in Gauna and its irritating consequences – really disgusted the boys. It was rumoured that they planned to give him a 'therapeutic treatment' and that the Doctor restrained them. That was perhaps an exaggeration or an invention. The truth is that they had never considered Gauna as one of them and that they now consciously regarded him as a stranger. Their common friendship with Larsen, their respect for Valerga, fearsome protector of them all, prevented them from showing these feelings. And so, outwardly, relations between Gauna and the group did not change.

VII

The garage was a corrugated-iron shed situated in calle Vidal, a few blocks from parque Saavedra. As Señora Lambruschini said, the place was a furnace in summer, and in winter, when the corrugated iron became a virtual sheet of ice, the cold was indescribable. In spite of that, Lambruschini's workers always stayed. No doubt the customers were right: no one died of overwork in the garage. What the boss liked best was to sit and drink maté or coffee, depending on the time of day, and to let the boys talk. I think they respected him for that. He was not one of those boring people who always have something to say. He would poke around with his bombilla in the maté, and with his kindly red face, glassy eyes and nose like a huge raspberry, he would sit and listen. Whenever there was a silence he would ask absent-mindedly: 'What other news?' He seemed to be afraid that for lack of conversation he would either have to go back to work or get tired out talking himself.

Yet when he began reminiscing about his parents' house or the grape-harvests in Italy or his apprenticeship in Viglione's garage, helping to get Riganti's first Hudson in shape, he seemed a completely different man and he would talk and gesticulate away. The boys used to get bored but they forgave Lambruschini these moments, which were after all very brief. Gauna pretended to get bored too, though it did occur to him sometimes that Lambruschini's stories were really not all that boring.

That day Gauna turned up at one o'clock and asked for

the boss, to apologize for being so late. He found him squatting on the ground, drinking a cup of coffee. Before he could speak, Lambruschini said: 'You really missed something this morning. A customer came in with a Stutz and he wants us to get it ready for the National.'

Gauna could not summon up any interest. Everything, that afternoon, got on his nerves.

He left work shortly before five. He rubbed his hands and arms with a little petrol and then, with a piece of yellow soap, washed his hands, feet, neck and face; in front of a bit of mirror he combed his hair carefully. While dressing he realized the wash in cold water had made him feel better. He would go straight to the Platense and talk to the boys. Suddenly he felt very tired. He was no longer interested in what had happened the night before. He wanted to go home and sleep.

VIII

He went into the main room of the Platense, which was famous for the large glass globes of its lights which hung from long cords covered in flies. The boys were not there. He found them in the billiard-room. As Gauna opened the door, Maidana was preparing to do a cannon. He was wearing a very close-fitting almost violet suit, and he had a large, gauzy, white silk handkerchief round his neck. A middle-aged man in mourning, known as the Black Cat, was about to write on the little board. Maidana must have made his shot hurriedly because, although it was an easy one, he missed. They all burst out laughing. Gauna sensed a vague feeling of general hostility. Maidana recovered his self-possession and made excuses.

'The hand of the champion is obedient, but it seems to be jealous.'

Gauna heard Pegoraro say: 'What do you know? The Saint has just appeared...'

'Saint?' said Gauna, but without getting annoyed. 'Saint enough to give you the last rites.'

He realized that investigating the events of the previous night would not be as easy as he had imagined. He felt no great desire to make investigations, nor did he feel any great curiosity.

They had all been watching the game when, unexpectedly, he had walked in. Although their surprise was explicable, Gauna wondered whether the explanation might not be different once he knew what had happened the night before.

27

If he wanted the boys to tell him anything, he would have to proceed with great care. It would be a mistake to go away now, even more to start asking questions. He must simply stay there. As with certain illnesses, it was just a question of waiting. He was acutely aware that he was not taking part in the conversation. It was the first time this had happened when he was with the boys – or the first time he had realized it was happening. He told himself: 'I won't leave till seven.' He was a witness, but a witness with nothing to testify. Then it occurred to him: 'Massantonio stays open till eight. I'll go and see him then. I won't go at seven, I'll go at a quarter to eight.' He felt a secret pleasure in overruling his own decision, even more pleasure than in finding himself in the unexpected role of spying on his friends.

IX

As the barber's metal shutter was already down, he went in by the side door. At the back he could see a vast, abandoned yard with a poplar and a bare brick wall. It was getting dark.

He opened the inner door and called out. The land-lord's maid – Massantonio rented the place from Señor Lupano – told him to wait a moment. Gauna glimpsed a bedroom with a walnut-veneer bed, a sky-blue bedspread and a black celluloid doll, a wardrobe of the same wood as the bed, in whose mirror the doll and the bedspread were reflected, and three chairs. The girl did not come back. Gauna heard the sound of corrugated iron rattling on the far side of the yard. He took a step backwards and had a look. A man was climbing over the wall.

A moment later he called out again. The girl asked whether Señor Massantonio had appeared yet.

'No,' said Gauna.

The girl went and called him again. She came back after a moment. 'I can't find him now,' she said, perfectly naturally.

X

That evening they did not get together with Valerga.
Despite his exhaustion, Gauna wondered about visiting
him but then reflected that he had better not do anything
out of the ordinary, anything that would attract attention,
if he wanted them to help him unravel the mystery of the
lakes.

On Wednesday an unknown female voice rang him at
the garage and fixed a meeting for that evening at half-
past eight, near some villas in avenida del Tejar where it
crosses Valdenegro. Gauna wondered whether he was
going to meet the girl of the other evening; then immediately he thought not. He was not sure whether to go or
not.

At nine he was still alone in the deserted spot. He went
home to dinner.

Thursday was the day they usually met Valerga. When
he got to the Platense, the Doctor and the boys were
already there. The Doctor greeted him warmly but paid
no attention to him after that. In fact he did not pay
attention to anybody except Antúnez. He had heard that
Antúnez was a famous singer and he claimed he was hurt
(joking no doubt) that Antúnez had not judged 'this poor
old man' worthy of a recital. Antúnez was very nervous,
very flattered and very scared. He did not want to sing.
He preferred to deprive himself of the pleasure of singing
rather than expose himself in front of the Doctor. But the
Doctor would not give up. When at last, after a lot of
persuasion and endless excuses, Antúnez, trembling with

nerves and anticipation, began to clear his throat, Valerga said: 'I'll tell you what happened to me once with a singer.'

It was a long story, almost all those present were interested, and Antúnez was forgotten. Gauna decided that if things did not arise naturally, he should not ask the Doctor's advice about his affair.

XI

That night, while he was eating some stale bread, curled up in bed and shivering with cold, he reflected that every man's soltitude was absolute. He was convinced that the experience of the lakes had been magical and that perhaps for that very reason all his friends except Larsen would try to hide it from him. Gauna felt quite determined to see what he had glimpsed that night and to regain what he had lost. He felt more adult than the boys, perhaps more than even Valerga himself; but he did not dare to confide in Larsen. Larsen's common sense was invincible and he was also too cautious.

So he naturally felt very alone.

XII

A few days later Gauna went to the barber's in calle Conde to get his hair cut and when he went in he found a new barber there.

'Where's Massantonio?' he asked.

'He's gone,' the unknown barber told him. 'Didn't you see the sign in the window?'

'No.'

'Well, so much for publicity! Come with me.'

They went outside and the barber pointed to a notice that said: *Under new management. Complete transformation*.

'What's the transformation?' asked Gauna as they went back inside.

'Well, I couldn't very well put: *Under new management. Huge reductions*.'

Gauna asked again: 'What's happened to Massantonio?'

'He's gone to Rosario with his wife.'

'For good?'

'I think so. I was on the look-out for a barber's shop and I was told: "Pracánico, there's a barber's shop going in calle Conde, just the thing, and the owner wants to sell." To tell you the truth, he sold it pretty cheaply. Do you want to know what I paid?'

'Why did Massantonio sell?'

'I don't know for sure. They told me that one of those boys – there's no shortage of them these days – had got him marked out. First he forced him to go to the carnival.

33

Then he tracked him down here. I was told that if Massantonio hadn't jumped over the wall, he'd have been done in in his own barber's shop. Don't you want to know what I paid?'

Gauna stood lost in thought.

XIII

Then there was the evening when Pegoraro got drunk at the Platense. Someone was making jokes about the heat and the advisability of warming oneself up with grappa. To show his disagreement Pegoraro swallowed one glass after another. They were losing interest in the game of billiards and Pegoraro alarmed them all by proposing a visit to the Sorcerer Taboada. None of them really believed in the Sorcerer, but they were afraid that he might foretell something unpleasant, which would then actually happen.

'Fine way to waste money,' said Antúnez.

'You go in,' said Gomina Maidana, 'you put your cash on the table, they tell you a load of garbage you can't even understand and then you go away, more dead than alive. If something bad is going to happen, I'd rather not know, thank you!'

Larsen was particularly alarmed at the idea of going to the Sorcerer's. Gauna also thought it would be better not to go, though it did occur to him that he might find out something about his adventure at the lakes.

'The really modern man,' declared Pegoraro, taking another drink, 'has a consultation with the Sorcerer and then lives his life free of anxiety, in accordance with a programme that's clearer than a celluloid window-pane. The truth,' he went on, 'is that you lot are scared. In fact – what aren't you scared of?' He looked around in a provocative way. Then he gave a sigh and, as if talking to himself, added: 'The Doctor's got you in the palm of his hand.'

They left the Platense. Larsen had forgotten something; he went back in again and that was the last they saw of him. On the way Pegoraro asked Antúnez, alias the Pasaje Barolo, to sing them a tango. Antúnez cleared his throat a few times, said he had to assuage his thirst with a glass of water or a bag of gumdrops, sweet as a syrup, declared he was really worried about the state of his throat and begged to be excused. By that time they had reached the Sorcerer's house.

'A few years ago,' said Maidana, 'there were only one-storey houses and vegetable gardens here.'

They went up to the fourth floor and a dark-haired girl opened the door. 'Provincial,' thought Gauna. One of those girls with that narrow prominent forehead he hated. They went into a little sitting-room with some water-colours and a few books and the girl asked them to wait. Then, one by one, they went into the Sorcerer's consulting room. As the sitting-room was very small, when they came out they left the flat. They agreed to meet in the café.

As Pegoraro was leaving he said to Gauna: 'He really is a Sorcerer, Emilito. He guessed everything, without me taking my trousers off.'

'What did he guess?' asked Gauna.

'Well... he guessed I've got boils on my legs, and you know I do have a few.'

Gauna was the last to go in. Serafín Taboada held out a very clean, very dry hand. He was a thin, short man, with a great mane of hair, a high forehead, a bony face with deep-set eyes and a prominent reddish nose. There were a lot of books in the room and a harmonium, a table and two chairs. On the table there was a chaotic pile of books and papers, an ashtray full of cigarette ends and a grey stone that served as a paperweight. There were two engravings – of Herbert Spencer and Confucius – on the walls. Taboada asked him to sit down and offered him a cigarette (which Gauna did not accept). Then, after lighting one himself, he asked:

'What can I do for you?'

Gauna thought for a moment and then replied:

'Nothing. I've come to keep the boys company.'

Taboada threw away his cigarette and lit another.

'I'm sorry about that,' he said, as though he were going to get up and put an end to the interview, but he remained seated and went on enigmatically, 'I'm sorry, because I had something to tell you. Another time.'

'Who knows?'

'One mustn't despair. The future is a world that contains everything.'

'Like the shop on the corner?' said Gauna. 'That's what the sign says, isn't it? But when you ask for something you find it's always out of stock.'

Gauna thought that perhaps Taboada was more talkative than he was astute or intelligent. Taboada went on: 'Our destiny flows into the future like a river; that's how we imagine it down here. In the future everything exists because everything is possible. There you died last week and there you are alive for ever. There you have become a reasonable man and there you have become Valerga.'

'I won't allow you to sneer at the Doctor.'

'I'm not sneering,' Taboada quickly replied, 'but I'd like to ask you something, if you won't take it amiss: doctor of what?'

'*You* must know,' Gauna answered at once, 'because you're a sorcerer.'

Taboada smiled.

'Well said, my boy.' Then he continued with his explanation. 'If we don't find what we're looking for in the future, it is because we don't know how to look. We should always hope for something.'

'I don't have any great hopes,' declared Gauna, 'and I don't believe in witchcraft either.'

'Maybe you're right,' said Taboada sadly. 'But we'd have to know what you call witchcraft. Let's take thought transference for example. I can assure you there's no great skill in knowing what an irritated and frightened young man is thinking.'

Taboada's fingers seemed very smooth and dry. He was continually lighting cigarettes, smoking them a bit and then stubbing them out in the ashtray. Or else he would sharpen the point of a pencil on the striking-edge of a matchbox. There was no nervousness in these movements. He was not nervous as he threw away the cigarettes but absent-minded.

'How long is it since you came to the neighbourhood?' he asked.

'You must know,' replied Gauna and then he immediately wondered whether his attitude wasn't rather ridiculous.

'That's true,' admitted Taboada. 'A friend brought you and then you got to know other friends, perhaps less worthy of your trust. You went on a kind of journey and now you are full of a sense of loss like Ulysses back in Ithaca or Jason remembering the golden apples.' It was not the mention of the adventure that attracted Gauna but the fact that in the Sorcerer's words he glimpsed an unknown world, perhaps more alluring than the brave, nostalgic world of the Doctor.

Taboada went on: 'That journey (since we have to call it something) was neither entirely good nor entirely evil. For your own sake and for that of others, do not repeat the journey. It is a beautiful memory and memory is life. Do not destroy it.'

Once again Gauna had a feeling of hostility towards Taboada, and also of distrust.

'Whose picture is that?' he asked, to interrupt the Sorcerer's flow of speech.

'That engraving shows Confucius.'

'I don't believe in priests,' declared Gauna vehemently and then, after a pause, he asked: 'If I want to remember what happened on that journey, what should I do?'

'Try to get better.'

'I'm not ill.'

'Someday you will understand.'

'Perhaps,' Gauna admitted.

'Why not? If you want to understand, become a Sorcerer. Believe me, all you need is a little method, a little application, and the experience of a lifetime.'

With the aim of distracting Taboada, in order to return to the interrogation afterwards, Gauna pointed to the stone that served as a paperweight and asked: 'And this?'

'It's a stone. A stone from the Sierras Bayas. I picked it up with my own hands.'

'You've been in the Sierras Bayas?'

'In 1918. Incredible as it may seem, I picked up that stone on the day of the Armistice. So you see, it's a souvenir.'

'Nine years ago!' exclaimed Gauna.

He took courage, thought to himself: 'He's a poor old man,' and after a brief pause, he asked: 'On the subject of what you call my journey, shouldn't I continue my investigations?'

'One should never stop one's investigations, but,' the Sorcerer went on, 'what matters most is the spirit in which one investigates.'

'I don't follow you, Señor,' Gauna admitted, 'but, if that's so, why should I forget that journey?'

'I don't know whether you should forget it. I don't think you can. I simply think it's not a good idea for you...'

'Now I'm going to ask you a personal question and I hope you'll take it the right way. What do you think of me?'

'What do I think of you? How do you expect me to tell you that in a few words?'

'Don't get worked up,' replied Gauna softly, 'I'm asking you like the parrot who tells fortunes with bits of green paper: Will I be lucky or not? Is my health good or not? Am I brave or not?'

'I think I see what you mean,' replied the Sorcerer and then he went on absent-mindedly, 'However brave a man may be, he is not brave on every occasion.'

'That's true,' said Gauna. 'I saw a masked girl.'

'I know,' replied the Sorcerer.

Trusting him now, Gauna asked: 'Shall I see her again?'

'You ask me whether you will see her. Yes or no. I defended you against a blind god; I tore the web that was to have been woven. Although it is thinner than air, it will form itself again when I am not there to prevent it.'

Once again Gauna felt justified in his feeling of scorn

and resentment. Now all he wanted was to end the interview, and he asked as he got up: 'Have you any more advice for me?'

Taboada replied in a monotone: 'There is no advice to give. There are no fortunes to tell. The consultation costs three pesos.'

Pretending to be absorbed in something else, Gauna leafed through a pile of books and read foreign names on the spines including that of a count who must be Italian because, as well as another mistake, the word *conde* was spelt with a 't', and a title or surname that gave him the idea of writing a letter to the papers one of these days to set them straight, which he would sign 'Flammarion'. He put the three pesos on the table.

Taboada saw him to the door. Taboada's daughter was waiting for the lift. Gauna said: 'How are you?' but didn't dare shake hands.

As they were going down the light went out and the lift stopped. Gauna thought: 'Now's the moment for some suitable remark.' A few seconds later he stuttered: 'Your father didn't tell me it was my birthday.' The girl replied perfectly naturally: 'It's a short circuit. The light will come on again any minute.'

Gauna was no longer thinking of his reactions, his nerves, or of what he would say. He was aware of the girl's presence as one is suddenly, imperiously, aware of a palpitation in the chest. The light came on again and the lift went smoothly down. At the street door the girl put out her hand and said to him, smiling : 'I'm Clara.'

Then he saw her run to a car that was waiting by the pavement. Some boys got out of the car. Gauna thought the girl was going to tell them what had happened and that they would laugh at him. He heard the sound of laughter.

XIV

The first time Gauna went out with Taboada's daughter was a Saturday afternoon. Larsen had said to him: 'Why don't you put on your sandals and run over to the bakery?'

Neighbourhoods are like a big house where you can find anything. There is the chemist's on one corner, on another the shop where you get shoes and cigarettes, and where girls buy fabrics, ear-rings and combs, and across the road is the grocer's. *La Superiora* is fairly near, and the bakery is in the middle of the block.

The woman in the bakery served her customers impassively. She was a big, majestic woman, deaf, pale and clean, and she wore her thinning hair parted in the centre with large useless curls over her ears. When it was his turn, moving his lips in an exaggerated way, Gauna said: 'I'd like some cakes to go with maté.'

Then he realized the girl was looking at him. Gauna turned around; he looked. Clara was standing in front of a showcase containing jars of toffees, bars of chocolate, and languid blonde dolls .in silk dresses, filled with sweets. Gauna noticed her smooth dark hair and smooth dark skin. He invited her to the cinema.

'What's on at the Estrella?' Clara asked.

'I don't know,' he replied.

'Doña Maria,' said Clara, turning to the shopkeeper, 'could you lend me a paper?'

The woman handed over a carefully folded *Ultima Hora* that was lying on the counter. The girl leafed

41

through it, folded it back at the entertainments page, and read it carefully. She said with a sigh:

'We've got to hurry. Percy Marmon is on at half-past five.'

Gauna was impressed.

'Look – do you like this type?' asked Clara.

She showed him a picture in the paper, badly drawn, of a girl with almost nothing on, holding up a gigantic letter. Gauna read out: '*An open letter from Iris Dulce to the Judge of the Juvenile Court.*'

'I like you better,' answered Gauna without looking at her.

'How much do they pay you for your lies?' Clara said, pronouncing each word with emphasis. Then she turned to the woman. 'Here you are – thanks.' She handed back the paper and went on chatting to Gauna. 'You know, I once thought of working as a stripper but it's too complicated now if you're under age.'

Gauna did not reply. He realized that, inexplicably, he did not want to go out with her. Clara went on: 'I'm mad about the theatre. I'm going to work in the Eleo Company – it's run by a little guy called Blastein. He's hateful.'

'Hateful? Why?' asked Gauna with indifference.

He thought of the theatres he passed when he was downtown, of the stage door, of a glamorous life that went on until the small hours with women and red carpets, and ending in expensive drives in large open taxis. He had never suspected that the Sorcerer's daughter would initiate him into that world.

'He's hateful. I'm ashamed to tell you the things he says to me.'

Gauna asked immediately: 'What does he say?'

'He tells me his theatre is a sausage-machine and I go in one end like a slut' – the word made her choke slightly and blush – 'and come out the other more proper than a schoolteacher.'

Gauna felt a flush of pride and resentment come over him, a pleasant sensation that could perhaps be summed up like this: she would be his girl and he would show them how he could defend her.

He exclaimed, barely audibly: 'Slut. I'll break every bone in his body.'

'Or rather his freckles,' suggested Clara, seriously. 'He's got too many of them. But I should leave him alone. He's hateful.' After a pause she went on dreamily: 'I'm the Lady from the Sea, you know. It's a play by a Scandinavian, a foreigner.'

'And why don't they put on plays by Argentine playwrights?' asked Gauna aggressively.

'Blastein is hateful. The only thing he cares about is art. If you could just hear him talk.'

Gauna went on: 'If I were the government, I'd make everyone put on plays by Argentine playwrights.'

'That's what we say to an idiot who plays the part of an old schoolteacher of a girl called Boleta,' agreed Clara. Then, smiling, she added: 'But don't think old freckleface is as bad as all that. How he loves talking about clothes! He's a real character.'

Gauna looked at her wearily. They walked on a little way in silence and then parted.

'Don't make me wait,' Clara warned him. 'Meet me in twenty minutes at the street door. No, not just at the door, halfway down the block.'

Gauna felt a certain pity for the girl, as he reflected that all these precautions were useless because he was not going to pick her up. Or was he? He went sadly into his house.

Larsen said to him: 'I thought you'd died. Just as well I didn't put the water on to boil when you were out.'

Gauna said: 'I'll need a little water to shave.'

Larsen looked at him with a certain curiosity. He fixed up the Primus and the water and then examined the contents of the packet Gauna had brought. He selected a cake with burnt sugar on top, took a bite and remarked appreciatively: 'Look, let's forget about our great extravagant schemes and don't let's change bakery. That woman's really good.'

Gauna put a blade in his razor and hung the mirror up near the door to get more light.

'Shave later,' said Larsen, while he prepared the maté.

'Don't miss the fresh brew.'

'I'm going to miss it all,' replied Gauna. 'I've got to rush.'

His friend began drinking in silence. Gauna felt very sad. Years later he said that at that moment he remembered what he'd heard Ferrari say: 'You live in peace with your friends until a woman appears, that great intruder who carries all before her.'

XV

When they came out of the cinema, Gauna suggested:
'Let's go and and have some Uruguayan cherries at the
Argonauts.'

'I'm sorry, I can't,' replied Clara. 'I've got to have an
early dinner.'

First he felt distrust and then resentment. He said in a
hypocritical little voice that the girl did not recognize:

'Are you going out tonight?'

'Yes,' answered Clara ingenuously. 'There's a
rehearsal.'

'You must enjoy that,' remarked Gauna.

'Sometimes. Why don't you come and see me?'

'I don't know,' he replied, surprised. 'I don't want to
bother you. But if I'm invited, I'll come.' He immediately
added with false sincerity, 'I'm keen on the theatre.'

'If you've got a piece of paper, I'll write the address.'

He found some paper – a corner of the cinema
programme – but neither of them had a pencil. With her
lipstick Clara wrote: Freyre 3721.

How many times in the future would he come upon that
slip of paper unexpectedly – in the pocket of some
forgotten pair of trousers at the bottom of a trunk, or
between the pages of the *History of the Girondins* (a work
for which Gauna felt great respect because it had been
bequeathed to him by his parents, and which he had
actually started to read more than once), or in some even
less likely place? It was like a talisman of varying potency,
a sign that said to him: 'This is where it all began.'

Around ten o'clock it was drizzling. Gauna walked quickly, glancing from the slip of paper to the numbers on the doors of the houses and back again. He thought he was lost. He was not sure what he expected No 3721 to be, but he was surprised when it turned out to be a shop. A sign said: *The Lebanon of Argentina. A. Nadín, haberdasher.* There were two doors. One was covered with a metal blind, with on each side of it shop-windows also covered with metal blinds. The other was of varnished wood, with a little grille in the middle and large wrought-iron studs. He rang the bell on the wooden door, although it was the other one which bore the number 3721.

A few moments later a bulky man came to the door. In the dim light Gauna made out two dark curves of eyebrows and some marks on his face. The man asked: 'Are you Señor Gauna?'

'Yes,' said Gauna.

'Come in, my dear friend, come in; we were expecting you. I am Señor A. Nadín. What do you think of this weather?'

'Awful,' replied Gauna.

'Quite mad,' agreed Nadín. 'I don't know what to make of it. There wasn't much to be said for it before, but however bad it was at least you could be prepared for it. Now, on the other hand...'

'Now it's all upside down,' declared Gauna.

'Exactly, my dear friend, exactly. Suddenly it's cold and then suddenly it's hot, and yet people are surprised if you go down with flu or get rheumatism.'

They went into a little hall with a mosaic floor, lit by a lamp with a bead lampshade. The table the lamp was on was a kind of truncated pyramid, made of wood with mother-of-pearl inlay. On the wall there was the coat of arms of Argentina, two clasped hands, with rings on the fingers and with cuff-links, and a picture of the historic embrace of San Martín and O'Higgins. In a corner was a painted porcelain statuette of a girl; a dog was lifting up her skirt with his muzzle. Gauna resigned himself to contemplating the enormous bulk of Nadín. His eyebrows were very dark, very bushy and very curved and his face was covered with marks of the most varied shades of black and brown. Something about his lower jaw gave him the satisfied expression of a pelican. He must have been about forty. He spoke as if he were licking the bottom of a pan of dulce de leche and explained:

'We must hurry. The rehearsal has begun. The actors are excellent, the play sublime; but Señor Blastein is going to kill me.'

He took a red handkerchief from his back trouser-pocket, saturating the air with the smell of lavender, and wiped his lips with it as if it were a napkin. His mouth seemed to be permanently wet.

'Where's the rehearsal?' asked Gauna.

Nadín did not stop to answer but murmured plaint-ively: 'Here, my dear Señor, here. Follow me.'

They went out into a courtyard. Gauna repeated his question: 'Where are they going to put on the play?'

Nadín's voice was now almost a groan: 'Here. You will see it with your own eyes.'

'So this is the theatre,' thought Gauna, smiling to himself. They came to a large shed with a whitewashed front and zinc walls and roof, and opened a sliding door. Inside, a discussion was going on between some people sitting down and two actors standing on a huge table, with violet-coloured panels at the side that extended out to the walls. This table, which served as the stage, was com-pletely bare. The corners of the room were piled high with boxes of merchandise. Nadín showed Gauna to a seat and left.

One of the actors on the table or stage was carrying a woman's coat over his arm and explained: 'Elida has to have this coat on; she's come back from the beach.'

'What's the connection between the fact that Elida's come back from the beach and this ineffable object with its drooping sleeves, its belts and epaulettes?' shouted a little man with a face covered in freckles and a mass of straw-coloured hair that stood up on end.

'Don't get worked up about it,' recommended a second character (he was dark, with a two days' growth of beard, wore a milkman's jacket, had a cigarette scornfully between lips sticky with dried saliva and held the text of the play in his hand). 'The author wants the coat. Just take the trouble to read. It's printed here: "Elida Wangel appears beneath the trees near the poplar grove. She has thrown a coat over her shoulders; her hair is loose and still wet."'

Nadín reappeared with more spectators, who sat down. The man with the hair standing on end leapt on to the platform, seized the coat and waving it around, yelled:

'Are you trying to crucify Ibsen with these realistic sleeves? A cloak is all we need. Or something that suggests a cloak. Remember that we want to stress the magical side. In fact Elida is a girl who has seen the sea from a lighthouse, and above all has known a sailor, a bad character. Perversity attracts women. Elida is permanently marked by it. That is the story, according to the bible that Antonio's waving around,' he pointed to the man with the text. 'But who can be so hard-hearted as to leave a genius alone? No, we have to give him a helping hand. So, in *our* play, Elida is a mermaid, as she is in the scene with Ballested. She has come mysteriously from the sea. She has married Wangel and they have established a happy home. Or rather, everyone knows that there is happiness in their home. But they are not actually happy because Elida is fading away, spellbound by the call of the sea.' He paused and then added: 'I'm fed up with talking to puppets.' With one bound he leapt down from the stage: 'On with the rehearsal!'

The actors began rehearsing again without a break. One of them said: 'Life in the lighthouse has left indelible traces. No one here understands her. They call her the lady from the sea.'

The other actor replied with exaggerated surprise: 'Is that true?' Antonio, the little man with the text, lost his temper.

'But where are you going to get the cloak from?'

'From here,' shouted the man whose hair stood on end, in a fury, making straight for the boxes.

The enormous Señor Nadín rushed up, waving his

arms and proclaiming: 'I've given you my life, my house, my shed! But not my merchandise. That is *not* to be touched.'

Calmly, Blastein began opening the boxes and asked: 'Where shall I find some yellow material?'

'This man will be the death of me,' wailed Nadín. 'The merchandise is *not* to be touched.'

'I asked you where you're hiding the yellow material,' repeated Blastein implacably.

He found it, asked for some scissors (which Nadín handed over with a sigh), measured two lengths and began cutting savagely and carelessly.

On seeing his material being torn up, Nadín rocked his head to and fro, holding it in his two enormous hands, bespangled with green and red rings.

'It's chaos here,' he shouted. 'How can I stop my assistant's petty thefts now?'

Waving the material like a golden flame, Blastein returned to the stage.

'What are you doing here, rooted to the ground, staring at me like two pillars of salt?' he asked the actors.

He leapt on to the stage with one bound and promptly disappeared behind the violet panels. The rehearsal continued. Suddenly, with excitement, Gauna heard Clara's voice. The voice asked:

'Wangel, are you there?'

One of the actors replied: 'Yes, my beloved.' Clara emerged from behind the panels, the yellow cloak over her shoulders and the actor held out his hands to her, exclaiming with a smile: 'Here is the mermaid.'

Clara stepped forward lightly, took his hands and said: 'At last I have found you. When did you arrive?'

Gauna watched the rehearsal with rapt attention, his mouth half-open and with mixed feelings. He was still conscious of his initial disillusion, like a faint, prolonged echo. It had been like being humiliated in front of himself. 'How could I not have suspected,' he thought to himself, 'when they told me the theatre was in calle Freyre?' But now, puzzled and proud, he saw the Clara he knew transfigured into the unknown Elida. His abandon-

49

ment to the enjoyment – a kind of smug, marital enjoyment – would have been complete but for the fact that the impassive, attentive masculine faces watching the performance suggested to him that she could be snatched away from him by some inevitable chain of circumstances, or left to him, apparently untouched, but stained by lies and treachery.

Then he noticed that the girl was greeting him with a look of trusting happiness. The rehearsal had stopped and they were all holding forth in loud voices about the play or the acting. Gauna felt he was the stupidest; only he had nothing to contribute. Clara, resplendent with youth, beauty and a new superiority, got down from the stage and came towards him, looking at him in a way that seemed to eliminate the others, leaving only him to receive the homage of her open, wholehearted affection. Blastein stepped in between them. He was pulling by the arm a sort of blond giant, clean and pink-faced as though he had just emerged from a boiling-hot bath. His clothes were brand new and the general effect was of a profusion of cardigans, flannels and pipes in shades of grey and brown.

'Clara,' exclaimed Blastein, 'allow me to introduce my friend Baumgarten, a new recruit to the profession of theatre critic. If I've understood him aright, in the Health Workers' Union Club, he's a friend of the nephew of a photographer on the magazine *Don Goyo* and he's going to publish a short review about our effort.'

'That's lovely,' she replied, smiling at Gauna, who took her by the arm and led her away from the group.

XVI

In the evenings he went with her to rehearsals. He also met her in the late afternoons when he finished work, and if there was no rehearsal they would go for a walk in the park. Several days went by like this and when Thursday came he was not sure whether to see Clara or go to Dr Valerga's house. Finally he decided to tell her he could not see her that evening. Without concealing her disappointment, the girl immediately accepted Gauna's explanation.

Larsen and he arrived at the Doctor's house around ten o'clock. Antúnez, alias the Pasaje Barolo, was talking about economics, the criminal rate of interest that some money-lenders, veritable blots on their profession, were demanding, and of the 40 per cent profit he would make if he managed to turn his ambitious plans and dreams into reality. Looking at Gauna, Dr Valerga explained: 'Our friend Antúnez, whom you see here before you, has great schemes. He is attracted by the world of commerce and would like to open a greengrocer's in the market.'

'But the enterprise is a non-starter,' intervened Pegoraro. 'The poor boy has no capital.'

'Maybe Gauna could chip in with his little sum,' suggested Maidana, shrinking obsequiously, and smiling.

'Even if it was only *sum*bolic,' added Antúnez, as though wanting to turn it all into a joke.

Dr Valerga looked Gauna in the eyes very seriously and leant slightly towards him. The boy said afterwards that at that moment he felt as though the Municipal Waterworks

Building, that great pile that was brought from England by boat, was falling on top of him. Valerga asked:

'How much have you got left after that wild carnival, little one?'

'Nothing!' replied Gauna, angry and indignant. 'There's nothing left at all.'

They let him finish protesting, then he calmed down; his voice trailed away feebly: 'not even a miserable five-peso note.'

'Five hundred, don't you mean?' corrected Antúnez with a wink.

There was a moment's silence. Then, pale with anger, Gauna asked:

'How much do you think I won on that race?'

Pegoraro and Antúnez both opened their mouths to speak, but Dr Valerga cut in quickly: 'That's enough. Gauna has told the truth. Whoever thinks otherwise can leave this house at once – even those who aspire to become slaughterers of vegetables.'

Antúnez began to stammer. The Doctor looked at him curiously:

'And what, pray, are you doing here, rolling your eyes like a sick sheep? Don't be a dog in the manger. Give us the privilege of hearing those cicada-like tones.' Now he spoke in the gentlest possible way. 'Do you think it is quite suitable that we should all be on our knees to you, and that you still keep us waiting?' Then, with a sharp change of voice: 'Sing, my boy, sing.'

Antúnez stared into space. He shut his eyes and then opened them. With a trembling hand he wiped his forehead, then his face, with a handkerchief. When he put it back in his pocket, his face seemed in some strange way to have absorbed the whiteness of the handkerchief. He was very pale. Gauna felt that someone, probably Valerga, ought to say something, but the silence continued. Finally Antúnez moved on his chair and seemed about to weep or to faint. He got up and said by way of explanation: 'I can't remember anything.'

Gauna whispered quickly: *'He was a tiger for the tango.'*

52

Antúnez looked at him without seeming to understand. Again he wiped his face with his handkerchief and passed it once more over his parched lips. With difficulty, stiffly, with agonizing slowness, he opened his mouth. The song flowed out with languorous sweetness:

> *Why leave me here sighing,*
> *My Julián fair?*
> *Your beloved is dying*
> *Of pain and despair.*

Gauna told himself he had made a mistake: how could he have suggested that tango to poor Antúnez? The Doctor would surely not let slip this opportunity for more teasing, and he foresaw with a feeling bordering on weariness the jokes that were coming – 'Tell us the truth, now, dear boy – who is your fair Julián?' and so on. He looked up, resigned. But Valerga was listening, in a state of innocent bliss. After a moment, however, he got up and beckoned to Gauna to follow him. The singer stopped.

'You don't have much staying power, do you?' said the Doctor sarcastically. 'If you don't carry on singing till we come back, I shall deprive you of your desire to be a human gramophone.' He turned to Gauna: 'He's so sickly sweet, he should play the violin in a brothel.'

Antúnez launched into *Mi Noche Triste*; the boys stayed where they were, listening to him, and Gauna, with faltering assurance, followed Valerga, who led him into the room next door. It had a little pine table in it, a wardrobe of pale varnished wood, a bed covered with grey blankets, two chairs with rush seats and – what seemed an inconsistency, an almost effeminate luxury amid such austerity – a Viennese armchair. Hanging in the middle of a wall with peeling plaster was a small, round, framed, unglazed, fly-blown photograph of the Doctor, taken in his unimaginable youth. On the pine table there was a bluish glass jug of water, a jar of Napoleon maté, a sugar bowl, a maté gourd with a silver rim, a bombilla decorated with gold and a tin spoon.

The Doctor turned towards Gauna and, placing a hand

on his shoulder – which was an unusual gesture, because Valerga seemed to have an instinctive repugnance about touching people – he announced:

'Now I am going to show you a few of my possessions that I only show to friends, and I don't want any interruptions.'

He opened a box of Bellas Artes biscuits that he took out of the wardrobe, and emptied its contents on to the table: three or four envelopes full of photographs and some letters. Pointing to the photographs with his index finger he said: 'While you look through them, we'll have some maté.'

He took a little enamel kettle out of the same wardrobe, filled it with water from the jug and put it on to a primus stove to heat. Gauna reflected enviously that it was a good deal bigger than theirs.

There were many photographs of the Doctor, some with plants in vases, and balustrades, signed by the photographer, and others, less posed and less stiff, taken at odd moments by anonymous amateurs. There were also a large number of photographs of old people of both sexes, of babies (dressed and standing up or naked and lying down), all of them people completely unknown to Gauna. From time to time, the Doctor would explain: 'A cousin of my father', 'my aunt Blanche', 'my parents, on the day of their golden wedding', but for the most part he passed the portraits over for Gauna's scrutiny with no more comment than a respectful silence and a watchful look. If any photograph was added quickly to the pile of those already studied, he would say in a tone that was a mixture of reproach and encouragement: 'There's no rush, my boy. You won't get anywhere like that. Take your time.'

Gauna was very moved. He did not understand why Valerga was showing him all these things but he sensed, with a gratified wonder, that his master and model was honouring him with a solemn proof of esteem and perhaps even of friendship. His spontaneous gratitude had always been emotional and extreme but that night it seemed to him to be peculiarly intense, because he had the feeling

54

that he was not the man he had been before, not the man Valerga thought he knew, not a man with an undivided loyalty. Or perhaps he was. Yes, he was sure that he had not changed; but the important thing was that, judged by the demanding standards of the Doctor, he had changed.

After that they had maté, Gauna sitting on a chair and the Doctor in the Viennese armchair. They barely spoke. An outsider might have imagined they were father and son. And Gauna felt that too.

In the room next door, Antúnez began launching into *La Copa del Olvido* for the third time.

'We've got to shut him up,' Valerga said; 'but first I want to show you something else.'

He rummaged around in the wardrobe for a moment, emerged with a little bronze trowel, and announced: 'With this trowel Dr Saponaro laid the foundation-stone of the chapel around the corner.'

Reverently, Gauna took the object, and contemplated it in amazement. Before replacing it Valerga rubbed it briskly on his sleeve to restore the shine to the places where the boy had placed his clumsy, moist fingers. Valerga took yet another object out of that inexhaustible wardrobe: a guitar, but when, with obsequious haste, his young friend tried to examine it, Valerga pushed him away, saying: 'Let's go back to the study.'

Antúnez was singing *Mi Noche Triste*, perhaps with less animation than on previous occasions. Brandishing the guitar triumphantly, the doctor asked in a muffled and thunderous voice: 'Just what do you mean by performing alone and unaccompanied when there's a guitar in the house?'

They all, including Antúnez, responded with hearty roars of laughter, heartier perhaps because they felt that the tension had ended. One look at Valerga was enough to see that he was in a good mood. Free of fear, the boys laughed until they cried.

'And now,' announced the Doctor, pushing Antúnez aside and sitting down himself, 'you will see what an old man can do with a guitar.'

Smiling and relaxed, he began tuning it. From time to

time the opening notes of a tune could be heard through his sensitive and practised strumming.

Then he hummed softly:

Poor unhappy mother –
Sing a doleful tune –
Just sits drinking maté
All the afternoon.

He broke off to comment: 'No more tangos, boys. They're for gangsters and brothel violinists. Or,' he added in a harsher tone, 'for the slaughterers of vegetables.'

With an ecstatic smile and loving hands, calmly, as though time did not exist, he began tuning the guitar again. He amused himself with these melodies, which flowed effortlessly, till after midnight. There was a general feeling of cordiality, of friendly and emotional happiness. Before asking them to leave, the Doctor asked Pegoraro to bring the beer and glasses from the kitchen. They drank to the happiness of all those present.

They had not drunk very much, but their exhilaration was close to drunkenness. They left together and the sound of their footsteps, their songs and their shouts echoed down the empty streets. A dog barked, and a cock, which they had undoubtedly awoken, crowed ecstatically, imbuing the night with the rapture of dawn and distant fields. Antúnez went home first, then Pegoraro and Maidana. When they were alone, Larsen ventured to ask:

'Don't you honestly think the Doctor was a bit hard on Antúnez?'

'Yes, I do,' said Gauna, struck by how uncannily he and Larsen seemed to read each other's minds. 'I was just going to say the same thing myself. And what about that business with the guitar?'

'What a scream!' said Larsen, shaking with laughter. 'How the hell could the poor sod have guessed there was a guitar in the house? Did you know?'

'No, I hadn't got a clue.'

'Neither had I. But you must admit that his joke

56

about performing alone was pretty disgusting.'

Gauna was laughing so much he had to lean against the wall. He knew that Larsen disliked dirty jokes, and although he did not feel the same himself, he sympathized to a certain extent. And it did actually amuse him.

'And I must say, my dear friend,' said Gauna, 'to be absolutely truthful, I thought Antúnez performed better alone than Valerga with the guitar.'

This remark caused such hilarity that it sent them zigzagging along the pavement, bent double, almost squatting, shrieking and groaning. When they had calmed down a little, Larsen asked:

'Why did he take you to the other room?'

'To show me endless photographs of people I don't know and even the little bronze trowel that Doctor someone or other used to lay the foundation-stone for some church somewhere or other. You'd have had a good laugh if you'd seen me.' Then he added: 'The strangest thing of all is that at times Dr Valerga reminded me of the Sorcerer Taboada.'

There was a silence, because Larsen wanted to avoid talking about the Sorcerer or his family. The silence was soon broken and Gauna hardly noticed it. He preferred to abandon himself to the pleasure of experiencing once again their intimate, inevitable companionship. He reflected, with a kind of brotherly pride, that their combined perspicacity was far superior to that of each on his own, and finally, with anticipated nostalgia, in which he foresaw his destiny, he realized that these conversations with Larsen were like nourishment to his soul. He thought with a certain resentment of Clara.

He thought: 'Tomorrow I could tell her I'm not going out with her, but I shan't. It's not that I'm weak-willed. What reason have I got for suggesting meeting Larsen on a weekday? We can see each other when we've got nothing else to do.' Then, sadly, he said to himself: 'We see less of each other every day.'

When they got home, Larsen said: 'Frankly, at the beginning, I didn't like the look of things. I thought they were all going to play some dirty trick on you.'

'What I think,' said Gauna, 'is that they were trying to manipulate Valerga, but he saw what was happening and put a stop to it.'

XVII

The following afternoon Gauna was waiting for Clara in the Argonauts. He checked his watch against the clock on the wall; he looked at the people coming in, all pushing the silent glass door with an identical movement. Unbelieveable as it might seem, one of those vague men or one of those women (hideous when you looked at them really closely), would be transformed into Clara. In his turn, Gauna was, or thought he was being observed by the waiter. When this circling spy approached the table, he was temporarily banished with the words: 'I'll order later; I'm waiting for someone.' Gauna thought: 'He must be thinking it's an excuse to sit here without spending any money.' He was afraid the girl would not come, and that the waiter would gloat to find that he had been right. He was a man women make fun of, even going so far as to send them to the Argonauts to wait for them, and then not coming. Irritated by Clara's delay, he pondered over the life women impose on men. 'They alienate you from your friends. They make you leave work early, in a rush, so that everyone resents you (and so that one day when you least expect it you lose your job). They make you soft. You wait in cafés, wasting your money on cakes. Then they overwhelm you with sweet words and lies and make you listen open-mouthed to explanations that you'd rather not hear.' He stared at two enormous glass jars, with metal tops, filled with toffees and as if in a dream he imagined that he was being drowned in all that sweetness. Just as he was thinking with alarm that perhaps in his moment of inattention Clara might have come in, not seen him, and left, he saw her by the door.

He led her to the table, so busy paying attention to her and so lost in contemplation of her that he forgot his intention, formed during his impatient musings, of glaring triumphantly at the waiter. Clara ordered tea with sandwiches and buns and Gauna a black coffee. They gazed into each other's eyes, asked each other how they were and what they had been doing; and in his vague and tender feeling of concern the boy saw signs of a distant, unimaginable and perhaps humiliating future. At the same time as this thought was forming, everything already seemed urgent and clear. He asked:

'How did it go yesterday evening?'

'Very well. I didn't do much. They rehearsed some scenes from the first act. The one that gave them most trouble was the one when Ballested talks about the mermaid.'

'What mermaid?'

'A dying mermaid who has got lost and cannot find her way back to the sea. It's Ballested's scene.'

Gauna looked at her rather puzzled; then, as though making a resolution, he asked her: 'Do you love me?'

She smiled.

'How could I not love you, with those green eyes?'

'Who were you with?'

'With all of them,' she answered.

'Who saw you home?'

'Nobody. Guess what – that tall boy, the one who's going to write the review in *Don Goyo*, wanted to see me home but it was early and I still didn't know whether I'd be needed. He got tired of waiting for me and left.'

Gauna looked at her with a candid and solemn expression: 'The most important thing,' he said, taking her by the hands and leaning towards her, 'is to tell the truth.'

'I don't understand you,' she replied.

'I'll try and explain. You can get close to another person to amuse yourself or because you love them; there's nothing wrong in that. Then, one person hides something to prevent the other suffering. The other

60

discovers that something has been hidden but doesn't know what. The person tries to find out, accepts the explanations and conceals his or her disbelief. That's when trouble begins. I don't want us to hurt each other, ever.'

'Neither do I,' said Clara.

'But you must understand me. I know we are free. At least we're completely free now. You can do what you like, but always tell me the truth. I love you very much and what I value most is our understanding of each other.'

'No one has ever talked to me like this,' said the girl.

The gaze of her radiant eyes, dark and pure, made him ashamed; he felt he had been found out. He wanted to admit that this whole theory of freedom and frankness was an improvisation, a hasty memory of conversations with Larsen that he was now churning out in order to conceal his investigations, his need to know what she had done on the evening when he had not gone out with her, to attempt to disguise the unexpected and pressing feeling that was overwhelming him: jealousy. He started to mumble but the girl exclaimed: 'You're wonderful.'

He thought she was making fun of him, but when he looked at her, he realized she was speaking seriously, almost fervently. He felt even more ashamed. He realized that he was not sure he believed what he had said, nor that he aspired to a perfect understanding with her, nor even that he loved her so much.

XVIII

When Gauna got back after taking Clara home, Larsen was asleep. Gauna got into bed quietly, without turning on the light. Then he called out: 'How are you?'

Larsen replied in the same tone: 'Fine, and you?'

They chatted almost every night across the room.

'I sometimes wonder whether you shouldn't treat women like they did in the old days, as the Doctor says. Hardly any explanations, hardly any compliments, your hat pulled down over your eyes, and talking to them over your shoulder.'

'You can't treat anyone like that,' answered Larsen.

Gauna explained: 'Listen, I don't know how to put it exactly, but the same ideas don't work for everybody. I've come to the conclusion that you and I are too tolerant, and this can lead to humiliation and cowardice. We don't know how to contradict people: we immediately hoist the white flag. We've got to harden ourselves. Also, women corrupt you with their little attentions and acts of kindness. The poor things make you feel sorry for them; you can tell them any kind of nonsense and they listen to you open-mouthed, like a schoolgirl. Don't you see that it's ridiculous to come down to their level.'

'I wouldn't be so sure,' replied Larsen, half-asleep. 'They love to flatter you, but then when you're not expecting it, they run rings around you. And don't forget that while you're sweating away in the garage all afternoon, they're stuffing their heads with *Para Ti* and a pile of fashion magazines.'

XIX

Gauna watched another rehearsal. The actor who was playing the part of Wangel and Clara, as Elida, were on the stage. The man was declaiming: 'You cannot get acclimatized here. Our mountains oppress you and weigh on your soul. We cannot offer you enough light, breadth of sky, horizon, air and open space.'

Clara replied: 'That is true. Night and day, winter and summer, I feel the lure of the sea.'

'I know,' replied Wangel, caressing her head, 'and that is why the poor sick girl must return home.'

Gauna wanted to listen but the *Don Goyo* critic was talking to him:

'I want to explain to you very simply the problem of our theatre today. The new, young Argentine writer is stifled, suffocated, because he has no way of seeing his ideas realized. On the purely artistic side, I can assure you the situation is appalling. I, for example, could write an *auto sacramental*, something absolutely modern; a well-seasoned mixture of Marinetti, Strindberg and Calderón, stewed in the secretions of my precocious glandular system, on a wild, fantastic witches' sabbath. But what guarantee would I have? Who would put it on? I'd have to put pressure on all the companies or even threaten them with the mounted police. While the writer who is unknown, imperfect if you like, languishes on his couch and cannot give birth to his monsters, the pot-bellied public, that bourgeois god invented by masonic liberalism, lolls back in comfortable seats that cost a fortune, watching the plays that take its fancy, having chosen them, because that public is no fool, from among the best of the international repertoire.'

Gauna thought to himself: 'You may know a lot and you may have read a lot of books but you'd swap right now with an ignoramus like me, simply to go out with Clara.' Baumgarten went on:

'They tell me it's the same with publishing. Take my cousin for example, a boy just like me, good-looking, tall, blond and fair-skinned, healthy, of European extraction. He has an enquiring mind. He has written a book: *Tosko, the Giant Dwarf*. The well-known young artist Ba-Bi-Bu made a drawing of this character on the cover and signed it. The whole family has invested money in it and it's a beautiful book. It hasn't got many pages but they're big, they come up to here' – Baumgarten slapped his calf – 'with black lettering, like on a poster, and enormous margins so that the writing gets lost. Fine, well, you ask for it in a bookshop and they have to go down to the lower basement, where they find it in a bundle that came from the old printer Rano. You open a newspaper and plough through the books page and there's not a word, not a mention. It's a scandal. And if you do find a review, it could equally well apply to a collection of sonnets by some Corresponding Member of the Historical Academy. The latest fashion is for the signed review, the highbrow review, in the press. It is the moral and practical duty of our scribes to take the offensive. We must not sit back until every Argentine work is the object of the serious and above all sympathetic study it demands. My cousin sometimes terrifies his wife, by saying that he wants to give up writing.'

Gauna thought: 'Why don't you shut up for a moment? After all, that green cardigan, that thick woollen jacket, that pink, well-shaven double chin, which you no doubt share with your cousin and all the rest of your family, are not going to help you one little bit when it comes to going out with Clara after the rehearsal. And that is the only thing you really care about.'

His attention had wandered. He realized the giant was

64

no longer talking to him and he saw him standing near the stage. Clara was coming towards them.

'Am I to have the honour' – Baumgarten was saying with his most seductive smile, rubbing his hands as though washing them – 'of seeing you this evening and depositing you on the threshold of your abode?'

Clara replied without looking at him: 'You've already seen enough of me. I'm going out with Gauna.'

In the street she took Gauna's arm and clinging to him a little she asked: 'Take me somewhere; I'm awfully thirsty.'

They wore themselves out wandering all over the neighbourhood; no cafés or shops were open. Clara barely looked at them but went on about how thirsty and exhausted she was. Gauna wondered why the girl didn't resign herself to being taken back home; there'd be a tap with water to drink, enough even to bath in, and a bed on which to sleep, like a queen, until the Day of Judgement. Furthermore he was getting bored with women's whims. He was too exhausted to talk and wondered how he was going to feel the next morning, when he got up at six o'clock to go to the garage. Prompted perhaps by some memory of the book Baumgarten had mentioned, he wished the girl would turn into a dwarf five centimetres high. He would put her in a matchbox – he remembered the flies whose wings his schoolfriends used to pull off – and put that in his pocket and then go to bed.

'You've no idea how I like walking with you on a night like this!' said Clara.

He gazed into her eyes and realized he loved her very much.

XX

The following day there was no rehearsal. When he got out of work, Gauna went into the shop and rang Clara to ask her where she would like to go. Clara told him her Aunt Marcela had come up from the country and she might have to go out with her; she asked him to ring her back in ten minutes, by which time she would have talked to Marcela and would know what she was going to do. Gauna asked the shopkeeper's daughter if he could stay there a moment. The girl looked at him with her large pear-shaped green eyes; she had two thick plaits, was very pale, and looked dirty. In Gauna's honour she put *Adiós, muchachos* on the gramophone. Meanwhile the grocer was having a tedious discussion with a travelling salesman who was trying to sell him 'a very noble product, some felt slippers'. The grocer was studying his books and insisted that never once in all his twenty-five years behind the counter had he heard of 'filter slippers'. Innately careless of pronunciation, neither noticed any difference between the felt being offered by the one and the filter being refused by the other. Not being able to reach agreement, they went on talking, taking no notice of each other, but waiting for the other to finish before replying. Indignantly, but without haste, they went on contradicting each other.

Gauna rang Clara back and she said: 'I'm afraid that's it, my love. I can't go out tonight, but I'll be expecting you at the theatre tomorrow.'

Because of what happened later, everything that happened that evening is important, or assumed importance in Gauna's mind. On leaving the shop he went back home, humming the tango he had heard on the gramophone. Larsen was out. Gauna thought of going to the Platense to see the boys, or visiting Valerga, or doing either of those and continuing his investigation, so remote now and so forgotten, into the events of the third night of the carnival. At the thought of these plans he was disheartened, wearied and bored. He had no desire to do anything, not even to stay at home. That was how the free evening he had so longed for began.

His resentment against Clara welled up again. He reflected that he had lost the habit of being alone. In order not to stay there, gazing at blank walls, his head filled with futile thoughts, he went to the cinema. On the way, he again hummed *Adiós, muchachos*. On the corner of Melián and Manzanares he saw a little baker's cart pulled by a piebald horse; he crossed his fingers and prayed that all would go well with Clara, that he would solve the mystery of the third night, and that he would be lucky. Just as he was about to go into the cinema another cart drawn by a piebald mare came down the avenue and he was able to uncross his fingers.

He was in time for the last scenes of a film with Harrison Ford and Marie Prévost which made him laugh a lot and put him in a good mood. After an interval occupied mainly by children racing up and down, and the comings and goings of the ice-cream man, *Love Never Dies* began. It was a long saga of romantic love that continued beyond the grave, with beautiful young girls and noble, disinterested young men, who grew old as you watched and all gathered at the end, white-haired, hollow-eyed and leaning on canes, in a snowy cemetery. There were exaggeratedly good characters and exaggeratedly wicked ones, and a sort of frenzy of misfortune. Gauna left the cinema with a feeling of suffocation and of unease that not even the return to the outside world and the night air could dispel. He realized to his shame that he was scared. It suddenly seemed to him that everything was contaminated with sorrow and anxiety and that nothing good could be hoped for. He tried to sing *Adiós, muchachos*.

When he got home, Larsen was just going out. They went and had supper together in the restaurant where the tramway workers eat in calle Vilela. As always Don Pedro, the old French lorry-driver, called out as he sat down heavily in his chair: 'A fricandeau with eggs'. As always, from behind the counter, the owner asked, 'Water or soda, Don Pedro?' And as always, in a rasping voice and with the tone of a waiter, Don Pedro replied: 'With soda'.

They had nothing special to discuss that evening and Gauna began to talk about Clara. Larsen scarcely responded. Gauna felt his friend's silence and tried to win him over with a profusion of explanations, clarifications and justifications. He wanted to give a good impression of Clara, but was afraid of seeming in love and enslaved; so he spoke ill of the girl and saw to his annoyance that Larsen nodded his head in agreement. He talked a lot and he talked alone, and in the end he felt depressed and disgusted with himself. It was as though the frenzy that had impelled him to slander Clara, make his friend uncomfortable and reveal himself as unstable and a fool, had now abandoned him, leaving him empty and exhausted.

XXI

When he arrived at Nadín's house, Clara appeared in a light-blue dress and a little lilac hat. The Turk opened the door.

'You're the first,' he announced. His enormous black eyebrows curved sharply upwards; his smile threw up a mass of creases and spots and revealed his moist, red lips.

'Not even our dear Señor Blastein is here yet,' he continued. 'But don't you stand awkwardly out here in the passage. Go on into the shed. You know the way. It's driving me up the wall, trying to get this crystal set to work.'

As if he had suddenly remembered something of vital importance, for example to warn them against some imminent danger, Nadín turned round and asked:

'How do you explain this heat?'

'I can't,' said Gauna.

'Neither can I, but it's enough to drive you crazy. Well, I won't keep you. Go on through. I must get back to my crystal.'

Clara walked in front. Gauna thought to himself: 'I know all her dresses now – the black one, the one with flowers on it, and this light-blue one. I know the look in her eyes when she's astonished and there's a very serious expression in them, like a child; I know the spot on her finger underneath her gold ring, and the shape and whiteness of the nape of her neck at the roots of her hair.'

Clara said:

'There's a Turkish smell here.'

They got to the shed. Clara had some difficulty opening the door. Gauna watched her. There was something very noble in the young girl's face as she bent over the heavy door-handle with an expression of genuinely thoughtful concentration. Then she bit her lip, gripped the handle with her two hands and pushing with one knee managed to open it. The effort made her flush slightly. Gauna went on watching her without moving. 'Poor little thing,' he murmured to himself, and an unexpected surge of compassion made him want to caress her head.

His mind went back to the time when he scarcely knew her even by sight. How impossible it had seemed that they should ever love each other! Clara only went out with smart boys from the centre of the city, who came and picked her up in their cars. He had always realized he could not compete with them. They belonged to another world, a world that he did not know and that was undoubtedly hateful. If he had tried to get off with her he would only have made a fool of himself and got hurt. Clara had seemed to him infinitely desirable, remote and prestigious, the most stunning girl in town, but quite beyond his reach. He did not even have to give up hope – he never had any. And now, here she was by his side, as exquisite as a little animal or a flower, or some small perfect object he had to look after and which actually belonged to him.

They went in. Clara switched on the light. Hanging on a wall was an enormous piece of parchment-like cloth, on which two masks were drawn in gold lines, with wide gaping mouths.

'What's that?' asked Gauna, pointing to the cloth.

'The new curtain,' Clara replied. 'A friend of Blastein's painted it. Don't those great open mouths make you feel sick?'

Gauna did not know what to say. The mouths did not make him feel sick, or anything else in particular. Suddenly he wondered whether this apparently pointless remark might not be explained by the urgent need we have all experienced at certain moments: the need to say something. The girl was nervous; he thought he could detect her hands trembling slightly. He thought with amazement: 'Can it be that I intimidate her? Can it be that I actually intimidate someone?' Again he felt tenderly towards her; he saw her as a little abandoned child in need of his protection. Clara was talking. It was a moment before he heard what she was saying. Clara had said:

'I haven't got an Aunt Marcela.'

Still preoccupied and still not taking it in, Gauna smiled. She insisted:

'I haven't got an Aunt Marcela.'

Still smiling, Gauna asked:

'Then who did you go out with yesterday?'

'With Alex,' replied Clara.

The name meant absolutely nothing to Gauna. Clara went on:

'He'd asked me to go out with him yesterday evening. I said no, because I never had any intention of going out with him. Then you rang up, and I knew that we'd go for the same old walk or to some film like we always do. I just felt fed up and it made me want to go out with the other guy. So I asked you to ring me back in ten minutes to give myself time to ring him and see if he still wanted to take me out. He said he did.'

'Who did you go out with?' asked Gauna.

'With Alex,' Clara repeated, 'with Alex. Alex Baumgarten.'

Gauna did not know whether to get up and strike her across the face. He remained sitting down, smiling, absolutely impassive. He had to maintain this absolute and above all apparent impassivity because his inner turmoil was growing. If he was not careful anything might happen – he might faint or burst into tears. Perhaps he had been silent for too long. He had to say something. When he spoke he did not worry about the sense of his words, simply the possibility of getting them out. He said the first thing that came into his head. He said:

'And this evening, will you go out with him again?'

He saw that the girl was smiling. She shook her head.

'No,' Clara assured him. 'I shall never go out with him again.' And after a moment, with a subtle change of tone that indicated, perhaps, that she was no longer thinking of Baumgarten, she added: 'I didn't like him.'

Like a sleeper who first dimly and then half-consciously hears the voices of the people around him, he heard the rapid chatter, laughter and shouts of Blastein, Nadín's daughter and the actors. Those who had just arrived stopped a moment, slapped them on the shoulders and greeted them. While all this was going on, Gauna was still smiling, feeling (and this was something that had never happened to him) that he was the centre of the scene. He wanted the people to go away; he was afraid they would ask him if he was ill or if something was the matter. Blastein exclaimed:

'It's late. Even Gauna, with that arrogant little grin of his, is impatient. We must get ready for the rehearsal.'

He jumped on to the table and disappeared behind one of the side-panels. The others followed him. Clara said to Gauna:

'Well, love, I've got to get ready.'

She gave him a quick kiss on the cheek and went off with the others.

As soon as he was alone, as though at a certain moment he had unconsciously made the decision, he fled. He went back to the door, crossed the yard, went along the corridor and out into the street.

XXII

He headed southwards, turned into Guayra and then left into Melián. He thought to himself: 'Ousted by that filthy wretch – that fat, flashy, well-scrubbed pig. And she still claims we're close to each other. If she likes that pig with his cardigans, if her tastes are as different from mine as that, how can she think we are close?' He smiled, amused by his thoughts. 'All women's tastes are different from mine.' He noticed that a boy was staring at him in amazement. 'No wonder – walking along the street laughing to myself.' He felt a magnanimous indifference, as though he had been drinking. 'As though I'd been drinking the wine of her dark treachery.' These words ought to have saddened him, he reflected, but for some mysterious reason nothing saddened him. He repeated aloud: 'the dark wine of her treachery'. He began to hum a tango. He heard himself humming *Adiós, muchachos*. He wiped his mouth with his hand and spat.

Perhaps the best thing would be to finish off the evening in the Platense. He saw in his mind the people who would be there: Pegoraro, Maidana, Antúnez and perhaps the Black Cat. He found himself muttering: 'If anyone wants a fight, I'll give him one.'(Since they were almost all friends, it seems strange that he should have had this thought.) In the café he would forget his worries. In order to forget he would become a different man, even more amusing than Don Braulio, the workman from the Water Authority. The vision of this evening of triumph, eloquence and temporary oblivion mortified him.

73

Then he thought he should have stayed at the theatre. 'They'll notice my absence. Not only Clara, but Blastein and the others too. Maybe Clara will explain; she's not like other women.'

'I don't care what those people know. They will never see me again, and neither will Clara. The worst would be that tonight, because I'm not there, she may go out with that filthy wretch again. No, that shouldn't bother me. The worst would be that she should come looking for me, waiting outside the garage or at the door of my house. The worst would be having to produce an explanation.' The thought of explanations depressed him profoundly. What he would have liked would have been to slap her twice on the face and then leave her. But he could never do that to her. He would never bring himself to give her such a shock. As soon as Clara looked at him all his aggression would drain away. 'This is what comes of being so friendly and reasonable. Bloody stupid. Pansy business – friendship with women.'

The road sloped gently down for a hundred metres or so, and then went on, as though submerged between trees. Gazing out over the indistinct sprawl of the city, that dusky vista of roofs, yards and foliage, Gauna felt the sort of yearning that one feels when one looks out to sea from the coast; he thought of other distant places; of the vast boundaries of his own country, and he wanted to go on long railway journeys, to look for work in the harvest, in Santa Fe, or lose himself in the province of La Pampa.

He had to give up these dreams. He could not leave without speaking to Larsen. And he did not want to speak even to Larsen about what Clara had done to him.

There was nothing for it but to go back and appear all affectionate and cheerful. 'Present a solid front, in which she can't spot the smallest crack and then little by little show my indifference and begin to withdraw from her. Little by little, without any hurry, with great finesse.' Thinking about this he exulted, as though he were witnessing his own prowess, as though he were his own audience. 'With great finesse, such skill that poor Clara never suspects that my leaving her has anything to do with the Baumgarten business.' To Clara it would seem as if he were leaving her because he had stopped loving her; not out of spite or because she had betrayed him or broken his heart. Gauna realized that he was very moved indeed.

There was no reason to ask her what she had done with Baumgarten. 'It's me, so sure of myself, such a man, and I'm the victim of the business, the one who is deceived. Almost the woman.'

Another possibility would be to wait for the swine in some deserted spot and pick a quarrel. 'If you want a fight, I can oblige you, with my knife in your guts right up to its horn handle. If only I can avoid looking an idiot in Clara's eyes. There's no hope of making Larsen understand all this. To him I should only be an utter lunatic.'

He went into a shop – a green house, a kind of little castle with crenellations – on the corner of Melián and Olazábal. Behind the counter was a sickly, filthy individual. With one hand wrapped in a damp rag, he was leaning on a metal tap, shaped like the slim neck and sharp bill of a flamingo, and was listlessly and mournfully contemplating a sink full of glasses. Gauna ordered a rum flambé. After the third glass he heard a guttural, piercing and seemingly diabolical voice repeating 'Try your luck.' He turned to the right and saw, walking towards him along the edge of the counter, a parakeet. Beyond, lower down, stretched stiffly on a little chair, practically lying on the ground, a man was reclining, looking up at the ceiling; parallel to the man, propped up against the back of an identical chair, was a box supported on a long pole. The parakeet went on saying 'Try your luck', kept on coming nearer, and was now almost beside him. Gauna wanted to pay and get out but the shopkeeper had disappeared through an open door into the dimly lit depths. The bird flapped its wings, opened its beak, fluffed up its green feathers, and swiftly sleeked them down again. Then it took another step towards Gauna. He went over to the man who was lying on the chair.

'Excuse me,' he said. 'Your bird seems to want something.'

Without moving, the man replied:

'He wants to tell your fortune.'

'How much would it cost?' asked Gauna.

'Not much,' said the man. 'For you, twenty centavos.'

He picked up the box and stood up with a sort of awkward agility. Gauna noticed that he had a wooden leg.

'You must be crazy,' he said, observing with disgust that the parakeet was nodding its head in a knowing way and preparing to perch on his hand.

The man swiftly reduced the price: 'ten centavos.'

He grabbed hold of the parakeet and placed it in front of the box. The bird drew out a green piece of paper. The man took it and handed it to Gauna, who read:

> *You'll get your wish and find what you are seeking;*
> *Alas, the gods will grant you what you pray.*
> *It is the wisest of all parrots speaking –*
> *Meanwhile, enjoy life's banquet as you may.*

Gauna remarked: 'I suspected it was a bad-tempered bird. It doesn't want me to have any luck.'

'You're not to say that,' said the man, flaring up. 'We both always want good luck for our clients. Give me the paper. Look, you can't even read. Doesn't it say here, in print, that you will find what you're looking for and get what you're asking for? What more can you expect for such a reasonable sum?'

'All right, all right,' said Gauna, partly convinced. 'But the paper says it's a parrot and it's a parakeet.'

'It's a parakeetoid parrot,' the man replied.

Gauna handed him a coin, paid for the drinks and left the shop. He went down Melián to Pampa, turned right and then went along avenida Forest. These neighbourhoods were not like his. Instead of small scattered houses, which seemed to him open and cheerful, there were secluded villas set within a mysterious pattern of gardens, of trees whose canopies met overhead and of formal fences. At the gates haughty men in uniform looked at him, he imagined, with suspicious disdain. They made him hot with anger, and he had a sudden longing to collect the lads from Saavedra, who were always ready for

76

anything, and rip into them ... The trouble was that the lads would not follow him. In this selfish age, public-spirited acts were left to the individual, and what could the individual do on his own?

He thought of his neighbourhood. For him the name Saavedra did not conjure up a picture of a spacious park surrounded by a moat and famous for its quivering eucalyptus trees, but rather of a small, empty street, quite wide, lined with low, irregular houses, bathed in the sharp, clear light of the siesta time.

Like a man who, during those nights of amazing architectural fantasies and interminable small hours that follow the death of someone beloved, allows himself to be distracted from his faithful agony by frivolous or forgetful thoughts, Gauna asked himself: 'What is all this?' He wanted to return to his sorrow, to his loneliness and to Clara.

The source of his misfortune, he saw clearly enough, lay in his own mistaken behaviour, but he also suspected that in some deep and obscure way the blame for it all was to be laid upon acts which could not apparently be linked to Clara's will: singing the tango *Adiós, muchachos*, for instance, or doing up his left shoelace before his right that morning, or, in the afternoon, letting his mind sink into the gloom emanating from that film *Love Never Dies*.

He wandered on like a sleepwalker, at one moment seeing nothing, at another concentrating his attention involuntarily upon a single object; as for example when, in avenida Forest, on an empty pavement, he gazed with the intentness of a painter at a stout gnarled tree whose foliage, green shading into blue, seemed to lean over in a cascade of delicate leaves, and wondered why it had not been cut down.

He continued westwards; he thought again of Clara; he found himself once more among low houses similar to those of his neighbourhood (but not the same, he told himself); he walked interminably along unknown streets; he reflected with a certain sadness that the days were already drawing in; he went into a café and had first one brandy and then another; walked on again and found

77

himself in an avenue which was Triunvirato and turned left.

Instinctively he longed to punish Clara and punish Baumgarten. 'The bloodier the row, the sooner I shall get over this resentment.' Although people would be bound to hear about his humiliation, he would be able to forget her. And he would have to forget her if he were to start his life again. The trouble was that at some inevitable moment, when his present emotion had faded, he would remember this day and what the girl had said to him. The worst thing about revenge was that it made the disgrace permanent. So that although Clara had deceived him, he would achieve little by beating her up or even killing her ... 'But,' he murmured to himself, 'if I could make her fall in love with me so as to be able to forget her...' Unfortunately, he would have to go back to her and follow the way of self-denial and hypocrisy. How much more satisfying – if less sensible – to slap her, first with the palm of his hand, then with the back, and leave her for ever.

He walked for a time which seemed endless; he skirted the wall of the cemetery of the Chacarita, crossed railway-lines and saw between the houses railway carriages; he passed timber-yards and brick-kilns and finally, self-absorbed, he followed calle Artigas, beneath dark trees which seemed to form a vault beyond the sky. He crossed more railway-lines and reached the plaza de Flores. He suddenly noticed that he was tired; he had to sit down, he had to go into a café or a restaurant and sit down and have something to drink. But there were too many people. There were so many people that he got fed up. He walked on; he saw a No 24 tram going past; he raced along the street and jumped on to it. He was going to stay on the platform as he usually did, but his legs were shaking – 'they were asking for a seat', as he expressed it to himself – and he went inside. He realized that luck was with him, because his tram was the kind with cane-covered seats; he lolled back comfortably, paid for his ticket, and, with a certain pride (like that which everyone feels when they see their name printed on the electoral roll), he read the sign: *Capacity: 36 passengers seated.* He took out of his trouser pocket a greenish packet of Barrilete cigarettes, lit one and smoked it in perfect tranquillity.

XXIII

While the tram made its way east and then south, Gauna
let his thoughts dwell on Clara and on Baumgarten. He
imagined himself beating up Baumgarten in front of
Clara, ill-treating Clara and then forgiving her. But he
could equally well imagine failing in this enterprise,
defeated by Baumgarten's superiority in weight, his greater
reach, or Clara's mockery. Dejected, he then pictured
himself spending the rest of his life in gloomy isolation, an
object of respectful consideration by the whole Saavedra
neighbourhood. The rhythm of the wheels in the tracks,
rising to momentary ecstasies as the vehicle accelerated or
turned a bend, seemed secretly to encourage his rumina-
tions. Gauna felt the full weight of his misfortune; he gave
in to self-pity; he convinced himself that there had never
been a case like his, and that if only he were provided with
a pencil and paper right there – plus the ability to write
music and play the piano half as well as the ugliest of his
female cousins – he could compose such a tango as
would, in the twinkling of an eye, make him the darling of
the great Argentine people and leave Gardel-Razzano
open-mouthed with admiration. But no, the world was
not going to change for him; his future was fixed – the
length of this tram ride and sooner or later his return to
Saavedra. Worse still, his own mind was not going to
change. Clara's betrayal, making him withdraw and seek
solitude, would always be there. His relationship with
Clara, a sentimental one but also one of understanding
and friendship, would be there, demanding a proper

explanation, a responsible and mature solution: reconciliation, oblivion, the abandonment of resentful pride. Larsen and the whole neighbourhood would be there, watching his shame with regret, surprise or contempt. To change all this would require some act of folly – not just an ordinary act of folly which would serve only to increase his humiliation, but an ingenious act of folly that would alter everything and leave people confused and distracted, so that they totally forgot the truly depressing spectacle. But he lacked the necessary imagination and felt that he was quite capable of doing something stupid and making himself look utterly ridiculous. Or maybe not. Maybe he lacked the impetus even for that. Two courses of action were left. One was to go back, to conceal his feelings, overcome the bitterness which at that moment was the only thing that mattered, and dissimulate, in order to live a separate inner life and prepare for vengeance in the remote future. The other was to look for a fight. That was the answer. After the fight everything would have changed. Not fundamentally, of course – it would hardly be more than a matter of nuance – but that was a great deal. A fight...with whom? The obvious person was Baumgarten, but it would have to be someone else, someone who could not be linked with Clara's treachery. He had to find some way of distracting people's attention and also diverting his own mind from the whole affair.

As the tram went lurching down a deserted street in Barracas, Gauna noticed a light shining out on to the pavement. He got up; by the time he reached the platform the tram was already at the corner. He glanced behind him. With a light, confident movement he jumped off, and walking slowly down the middle of the street, looking at the rails whose flickering bluish reflection struck a sudden disturbing chord in his memory, he reached the lighted entrance. The door was half-open; he went in without ringing the bell. 'There are too many people here,' he said to himself, 'I'd better go.' He was being squeezed between a man in mourning clothes and another wearing a baker's jacket. Making his way forward with difficulty, on tip-toe, he tried to see what was going on, thinking at the same time, 'I hope it isn't an accident and I get dragged in as a witness.' At that moment he felt a pressure on his arm. It was a small woman, no longer young, with excessively blonde hair and an excessively green dress. Gauna looked at her with interest. Her thick lipstick had run and the beauty spot on her cheek was a sooty smudge. In a strong foreign accent she said:

'Did you know we had a wedding on?'

'No, I didn't. I don't know anyone here,' replied Gauna.

'Well, you'd better come back tomorrow,' explained the woman, adding immediately, 'but now you've got to stay and join in the festivities. Come and have a glass of Zaragozano or El Abuelo wine and try some of the cake.'

With difficulty a way was made for them to the table with the cakes. There he was given some food and introduced to two serious-looking girls. One had slanting eyes and a cat-like face and talked a lot, with breathless exclamations. The other was a quiet, nondescript girl whose part in the conversation was limited to the mere fact of her presence, of being there, of her body being there beneath its modest, flimsy dress. Gauna heard vaguely that the girls worked in Rosario, and a moment later he found himself pondering on the rapid development of that Argentine Chicago, a much gayer city than Buenos Aires, and a place he hoped one day to get to know.

'Since we never go out,' the chatty girl was saying bitterly, 'it wouldn't matter to us if Rosario were the gayest place on earth.'

The foreign woman talked to him about the wedding.

'There are plenty of spiteful gossips who will say that this isn't a proper wedding because there's no priest and no civil ceremony. But what are weddings nowadays? El Pesado* is a good lad. Maggie will have someone to look after her medical cards and her official documents and that sort of thing. I don't see what more a woman can expect from a husband.'

---

*The Bore

She immediately gave Gauna another piece of cake and suggested that he should come and congratulate the bride and groom. He tried to make excuses but she carried him off through the crowd to the corner of the dining-room, where the newly-weds were receiving the congratulations of their guests – congratulations which (to show that they were all at their ease and that they knew how to behave on such occasions) took the form of risqué jokes and smutty *doubles entendres*. The bride was a pale girl, probably a natural blonde, with a round hat pulled down over her eyes, a very short dress and high-heeled shoes. The groom was a corpulent, grey-haired man; his black suit and excessive neatness suggested a peasant on a visit to Buenos Aires; his hands, by contrast, were small, smooth and well cared for. After paying his respects Gauna elbowed his way out on to the terrace. He felt he had to get some fresh air; it was so stuffy inside that he could hardly breathe. He felt himself break out in a cold sweat and for a moment thought he was going to faint. He was thinking to himself, 'Oh, how embarrassing, how embarrassing,' when he was distracted by the sobbing note of a violin. He finally reached the terrace, which was very narrow and paved with grimy red tiles. Plants with white or yellowish flowers were growing in pots and tins. The musician was standing in a corner, leaning against a thin iron column and surrounded by a crowd of onlookers. The foreign woman, her mouth almost in Gauna's ear, asked:

'What did you think of the newly-weds?'

In order to say something, Gauna said: 'The bride isn't bad-looking.'

'Come back tomorrow then,' said the woman, 'she can't attend to you today.'

With a vague hope of escaping from his companion, Gauna went up to the violinist. Something like a crown seemed to encircle his brow – a ring of small discolorations, scars perhaps, in the form of jagged marks. The man looked about thirty; he was bare-headed and his thin, flowing brown hair gave him a certain solemn, authentic dignity. His sorrowful eyes were open

unnaturally wide and a smooth, fine pointed beard com-
pleted his pale face. Beside him a dreamy child was
playing with a hat.

'Play us another little waltz, maestro,' asked Gauna
humbly.

Slowly, as if to ward off some terrible but inexorable
blow, the musician raised his arms, pressed himself
against the column in an attitude almost of crucifixion,
uttered a hoarse groan, recoiled in terror and fled,
knocking himself several times against the wall of the
courtyard. The child with the hat was roused from his
abstraction, ran towards him, took him by the hand and
dragged him towards the door. Gauna was puzzled, but
instead of wondering why the man had run away so
unexpectedly, he compared it with the desperate flight of
a bird that had once flown through his uncle and aunt's
window when he was a child in Villa Urquiza. He pulled
himself together, and noticed that people were looking at
him with suspicion, and also, perhaps, with a certain
deference. The woman evidently wanted to talk to him,
but for some reason or other she could not get a word out.
Before she could recover, Gauna made for the door; the
crowd stood back to let him pass, staring at him. He
reached the street, crossed to the opposite pavement, and
walked slowly away. When he had gone a couple of
hundred metres he looked back. No one was following
him. He continued on his way, and after a while he asked
himself what had happened. He could find no answer.
The tune and the words of *Adiós, muchachos* hovered on
his lips for a moment.

XXIV

When he got back to his room he found Larsen was asleep. Gauna got undressed in silence; he turned on the tap in the basin and held his head under the gush of cold water for a moment. He went to bed with wet hair. Though he shut his eyes he could see images: small, animated faces emerging from others, like water from a fountain. They gesticulated, disappeared and were replaced by others that were similar but slightly different. He remained like this for a period of time that seemed endless, lying motionless on his back, watching the drama that unfolded itself before his mind's eye, until he fell asleep, only to be woken up again almost immediately by the alarm clock. It was six o'clock. Luckily for him it was his friend's turn to prepare the maté.

Larsen said to him: 'You came in late last night.'

Gauna acquiesced vaguely, looked at Larsen, who was lighting the stove, and thought, 'He always finds reasons for disapproving of Clara.' He was on the point of explaining that he had not been out with her – of expressing it like this: 'so it wasn't her fault this time' – when he realized with annoyance that his first impulse was always to defend her. They washed their faces and necks in turn. By the time they had had their maté, they were dressed. Gauna asked:

'What are you doing this evening?'

'Nothing,' replied Larsen.

'Let's eat together, then.'

Gauna paused a moment at the door, expecting Larsen

to ask whether he had had a row with the girl, but since all we can hope for from our fellow men is blank indifference, Larsen said nothing and Gauna was able to get away, postponing any awkward explanation, perhaps for good.

Outside there was a very white light and a heat still and vertical, like that of midday. The noisy milk-cart, rounding the deserted corner, confirmed how early it was. Gauna took the shady side of the street and wondered how he could manage to avoid meeting Clara during the New Year celebrations. Christmas Eve, he now remembered, had been the hottest day of the year; he smiled to himself remembering those old prints showing Christmas scenes in snowy landscapes. When he went inside the garage he felt almost suffocated; there was no air, only heat. He thought: 'By two this afternoon this corrugated iron will be like an oven. This is going to run Christmas Eve pretty close.'

Squatting in a circle, Lambruschini and the mechanics, Ferrari, Factorovich and Casanova were drinking maté. Ferrari had thinning curly hair, light-blue eyes, a pale, clean-shaven face and a scornful expression. He always had a burnt stub stuck to his lips, and when he opened them revealed a few large decaying teeth and a dark hole. His body was thin and clumsy and his huge feet were splayed apart at a prodigiously obtuse angle. Whenever he was asked to do anything, he would stroke his feet – he was always stroking his feet for one reason or another, whether with shoes or without – and say morosely: 'Flat feet. Exempt from all duties.' Factorovich had brown hair, dark eyes, staring and bright, and a large, pale, oddly angular face, as if hewn out of wood, with huge, sharp-edged ears and nose. Casanova had skin so bronzed and shiny that it looked as though he had been varnished. His thick covering of hair came down to his eyebrows like a dark, tight-fitting stocking. He was short; he had hardly any neck, and gave the impression of being not so much fat as inflated; but his movements were gentle and agile. He was always smiling but was friends with nobody. People said that only somebody with Lambruschini's patience could put up with him.

They were talking about a trip to the country, to the house of a relation of Señora Lambruschini. The latter had invited them.

'We'll be leaving at the crack of dawn on New Year's Day,' she said to Gauna. 'We're counting on you being there.'

On the spur of the moment Gauna accepted, but after the others returned to their conversation he began to wonder whether he could go after all; whether it would be possible to spend New Year's Day without her.

'How many shall we be?' asked Lambruschini.

'I've lost count,' replied Ferrari.

'You're forgetting the most important item,' Factorovich interrupted, 'the vehicle.'

Casanova gave his view: 'The obvious choice is Señor Alfano's Broakway.'

'Customers' cars are not to be touched,' declared Lambruschini, 'unless on official business or on the pretext of testing them. We'll manage with the van.'

XXV

With a considerable effort of will he avoided the girl
during the next few days. On New Year's Day, at three
o'clock in the morning, he arrived with Larsen at the
boss's house. The van – an old green Lancia whose
bodywork Lambruschini had replaced with a cabin and an
open platform – was parked in the street. A few people,
whom Gauna could not identify in the half-light, were
already waiting by the van, leaning against the railings,
restless, either because of the delay or the cold. When
they saw them coming, they shouted down 'Happy New
Year', and the boys replied with the same words. Gauna
heard the unmistakable voice of Ferrari:

'Why don't you give the New Year a rest? You look like
idiots.'

They talked about the weather. Someone remarked:

'Isn't it incredible? Here we are freezing and shaking
like jellies but in a few hours we'll be sweating like pigs.'

'It won't get hot today,' declared a female voice.

'No? Wait and see. Christmas Day won't have been
anything by comparison.'

'That's just what I'm saying; the weather's crazy.'

'Come on – be fair. What do you expect? It's barely
three o'clock in the morning.'

Gauna decided to go into the house and see whether
Lambruschini needed any help in loading up the van. Did
this reveal a low, servile nature? he wondered. Gauna's
character was still in process of formation. He himself
recognized that he could be brave or cowardly, generous

or self-centred, just as resolutions or chance dictated, and that there was nothing fixed and solid about him. Lambruschini, Factorovich, the two women and the young boys appeared. There were New Year greetings and hugs. Gauna and Larsen helped load some spare parts for the Lancia, a few tools, a little case and a heater. Lambruschini, the woman and one or two of the boys got into the cabin; the others got into the open part at the back. The truck started to move before the hugs were finished; there were jerks, tumbles and roars of laughter. Amidst the confusion Gauna heard a voice very near him saying: 'Wish me happiness, darling.' He was in the arms of Clara.

The girl explained: 'I met Señora Lambruschini at the draper's. She mentioned the trip and I asked her for an invitation.'

Gauna said nothing.

'I've brought Nadín's daughter,' added Clara, pointing to her friend in the dark. Then, very slowly, she put an arm around Gauna's shoulders and drew him close to her.

They crossed the whole city, continued through Entre Ríos, headed for the country over the bridge at Avellaneda, and taking avenida Pavón, they made their way towards Lomas and Temperley and Monte Grande. Clara and Gauna, numb with cold, in each other's arms, happy perhaps, saw their first sunrise in the country. Around Cañuelas a car kept trying to overtake them and managed to in the end.

'It's an FN,' Factorovich commented.

Gauna asked: 'What make is that?'

'A Belgian car,' said Casanova, surprising them.

'There are cars from all over the place here,' observed Factorovich with pride. 'There's even an Argentine car, the Anasagasti.'

'If I were the government,' Gauna told them, 'I wouldn't allow a single foreign car into the country. With time they'd be made here, and no matter how lousy they were, people would buy them without a murmur, and pay a lot for them.'

They were all in agreement over this policy and were

adding fresh arguments when they were interrupted by the first puncture. After changing the tyre they continued on their way again. Then there were more stops and more changings of tyres. They checked the fuel pump, stripped it down, cleaned it and put it together again. After that they continued onwards through mud and over pot-holes until they finally reached the Salado River. This had to be crossed by ferry, a prospect which filled everybody, young and old, with the greatest interest. Larsen was convinced that the loaded van weighed too much and that the ferry would sink. Although the ferry-men assured him that there was no danger, he was still distrustful. Since no one would listen to him, he eventually had to accept the fact that they would make the crossing in one go, van, passengers and all. But he went on repeating, till they were utterly fed up with him, that he had warned them that he would not be responsible for the consequences, and that he washed his hands of the whole business. Even so, he did his bit conscientiously when it came to loading the van on to the ferry and making it secure, checking the fastenings and commenting on all the details in a loud voice. The children listened to him attentively. When they reached the other side in perfect safety he did not seem at all embarrassed by his earlier fears; they had simply vanished.

They had lunch shortly before eleven, in the shade of some casuarina trees. While the women got the food ready, the men made a fire a little way off and heated the water for maté. As it was hot they had a siesta after lunch.

It was nearly two o'clock when they set off again. They left Las Flores behind them and as they were passing la Colorada, Larsen said: 'Now we've got to pay attention.'

'That's right,' replied Factorovich, 'all we've got to do now is take the right turning.'

'First we've got to get to the bridge,' corrected Larsen.

They all looked nervously at the road ahead. The bridge appeared, they crossed it with a creaking of planks and beside them they saw the canal, dead straight and dried up. Larsen remembered the instructions.

'When we're opposite a eucalyptus wood with a fringe of cina cina trees, we take the left turning, leaving the wood and the main road on our right.'

'Don't get too excited,' Gauna advised him, winking at Ferrari, 'considering where we're going, the best thing we can do is get lost.'

'I vote we return home,' announced Ferrari.

'Aren't they horrible,' cried the Turkish girl.

'The wood, the wood,' shouted Larsen excitedly.

He could not make the most of his triumph, because Lambruschini quickly turned left and the wood was left behind. Larsen turned around to look at it. The Turkish girl remarked: 'He looks like the captain of a ship.'

'The pirate captain,' amended Ferrari.

They all laughed. The road, narrow at first, after an automatic cattle-gate, was no longer fenced, and in the end it was no more than a track between pampas grass in the immensity of the countryside. Clara kept pointing out horses, cows, sheep, the chimangos, the owls and the oven-birds to the children. These explanations seemed to annoy Larsen, who needed all his concentration to keep to the road. They got lost many times, came to villages, exclaimed 'Ave Maria', asked for directions and got lost again. They stopped every few minutes. Larsen and Lambruschini got out too and began persecuting guinea-pigs by throwing lumps of earth at them. Then they all had to wait for the boys to get back in. The others applauded.

'I'm going to throw it at Luisito,' said Clara.

'I'm going to throw it at the guinea-pig,' said Ferrari.

'You're worse than the children,' protested Larsen, fed up with them. 'You're more interested in chasing guinea-pigs than in finding the way.'

'If only the rain holds off,' exclaimed the Turkish girl.

The wind had changed and there were menacing grey clouds in the south. It was a solitary place. The tall pampas grasses were waving against a dark sky that now seemed very close. Clara must have felt particularly exalted because she squeezed Gauna's arm and exclaimed breathlessly: 'There's the river.'

They caught sight of it, canalized, between very green, very dark pastures, with banks of bare earth. The water,

91

calm and inscrutable, came into view at a curve.

Larsen shouted: 'There's Chorén's wood.'

They could see a few willows, some black poplars and the odd eucalyptus.

'How wonderful,' shouted the Turkish girl, with little leaps, cries and giggles. 'We've arrived.'

'If we stay here, terrible things are going to happen,' said Ferrari, with a shiver that was not put on. 'Let's go home.'

They stopped beside the wood, in front of a palisade made of old patched sections of fence and rusty barbed wire. Lambruschini hooted the horn several times. Two tawny sheepdogs, their heads held up high and looking almost human, greeted them, barking. But their fierceness soon evaporated; they peed on the wheels of the Lancia, wagged their tails and wandered off abstractedly. Lambruschini hooted again. An unmistakably Spanish voice was heard shouting: 'Coming, coming.'

A little, shabbily dressed man appeared. He was bald, wore glasses and had a big bushy moustache. His thin mouth seemed somewhat over-endowed with both smiles and teeth. He shook hands – his hand was stubby, stiff and rough – and said to each of them: 'Fine, and you? A Happy New Year.' He asked Señora Lambruschini: 'How are things going, cousin?' and kissed her on both cheeks. She seemed embarrassed. Showing his innumerable yellow teeth and with open arms, he invited them in.

'Come along in.' He spoke in an admiring tone: 'Leave the van anywhere you like. It'll be fine here,' he pointed to a little shed, made not of mud brick, but of wooden boards, sheets of tin and dust. I was expecting you for lunch. Or perhaps you don't bother about lunch? There's never any lack of food here, though there may not be much in the way of creature comforts.'

Señora Lambruschini tried in vain to interrupt him and get on with the introductions. While Lambruschini stayed with the van, the others went into the house. It was a low, gabled house, made of adobe. There were three doors at the front, one leading into the bedroom, one to a spare room and one to the kitchen.

'Do you think it's going to rain?' asked Larsen.

'I don't think so,' replied Chorén. 'There was a good wind but now it's turned southerly and with any luck that'll clean everything up.'

'That's lucky,' exclaimed Larsen.

'Yes, indeed,' agreed Chorén. 'Bloody awful luck, if you'll excuse my language. We've never seen such a drought.'

Wanting to appear a true countryman, Gauna asked how things were going on the farm.

'The cattle are all right,' replied Chorén, 'but the sheep are in a bad way. It must be the drought.'

This distinction between cattle and sheep made Gauna feel that although his family came from Tapalqué, he didn't really know much more about the country than his friends.

Lambruschini's wife had talked about her relative's orchard. Factorovich, Cassanova and the little boys took advantage of a moment's inattention on the part of the others to disappear in quest of the fruit trees. They found two or three peach trees with no fruit, a blighted pear tree and a plum tree covered with minute red plumbs. That night they were rather sick.

Gauna and Clara, Larsen and the Turkish girl also moved away from the others. After walking through the undergrowth, beneath the trees, they came to the stream. Gauna and Clara sat down on the branch of an aguaribay that was growing on the bank, and stretched out over the water. Clara pointed everything out to Gauna: the sunset, the various shades of green, the wild flowers.

He said to her: 'It's as if I'd been blind. You're teaching me to see.'

In the distance Larsen and the Turkish girl amused themselves throwing flat stones into the river so that they bounced once or twice on the surface of the water.

When they came back they were thirsty. Chorén found a jug, went to the pump and pumped two or three times. Ferrari came up to have a drink.

'Bitter,' he commented.

'Yes, bitter,' admitted Chorén cheerfully. 'But they say

it's good for you, and people flock from miles to drink it. Who knows? I've got ulcers and the doctor insists it's the water.'

When they were alone, Ferrari said:

'I hope I'll soon get ulcers. At least it'd keep me busy.'

And with a pensive expression, he caressed the sole of his shoe.

'You're hard to please,' declared the Turkish girl.

In the evening they had maté in earthenware bowls, and dry biscuits. Ferrari did not eat any; he found them too hard and salty, with a taste of earth. Later they ate mutton stew.

'Anyone who doesn't get ulcers will go down with the plague,' declared Ferrari.

Clara begged Gauna not to drink any wine.

'One glass,' he insisted. 'Just one to get rid of the greasy mutton taste.'

Other glasses followed the first. In the bedroom the two women slept in one bed and Clara and the Turkish girl on a camp-bed. The children slept on piles of straw and so did the men, but in the empty room. Ferrari said he was going to sleep in the lorry, but came back after a while. They did not see Chorén. Some said he slept in the kitchen, others outside under a sulky.*

The next day they had mutton stew for lunch and dinner.

'This man has never eaten anything else,' Lambruschini told them.

'I bet he's never seen a chick-pea in his life,' said the Turkish girl.

'If he saw an escalope milanese, with lemon,' said Ferrari, 'he'd cross to the other side of the road.'

'I shouldn't think he's ever seen a pavement either,' said Clara.

After that the women who were helping him in the kitchen persuaded him to make some changes in the menu. On the last evening they would celebrate with a barbecue.

---

*A two-wheeled one-horse vehicle.

In the afternoon, when they set off for a walk, Gauna said to the girl:

'We've been joking about the discomfort all this time, without realizing that these were the happiest days of our life.'

'Oh, but we have realized it,' replied Clara.

They walked on feeling tender, almost sad. Clara made him stop to smell the clover or the bitterer smell of a little yellow flower. Joyfully they reminded each other of the incidents of the journey and of the last few days as though they had happened a long time ago. With emotion, Clara described dawn in the country: it was as if the world had been filled with lagoons and transparent caves. When they got back to the house they were weary. They had loved each other very much that afternoon.

They thought Señora Lambruschini was looking at them with a strange expression. At a moment when the three of them were alone together, she said to Clara:

'You know my girl, you're lucky to be marrying Emilio. I've always thought that the only eligible bachelors up till now have been old men.'

Gauna was touched, felt ashamed of being touched, and thought that those words should make him want to run away. He felt infinitely tender towards the young girl.

They planned a rendezvous for that night. When everyone was asleep, they would get up, leave quietly and meet behind the house. Gauna had the impression that he had been seen leaving; he wasn't sure he minded if he had been. Clara was waiting for him with the dogs.

'Luckily I came out before you,' she said to him. 'You wouldn't have managed to stop the dogs barking.'

'That's true,' agreed Gauna with admiration.

They went down to the river. Gauna walked in front and held back the branches so that she could pass. Then they got undressed and bathed. He held her in his arms in the water. Radiant in the moonlight, yielding to love, Clara seemed to him almost magical in her beauty and tenderness, infinitely lovable. That night they made love beneath the willow trees, startled by a grasshopper or a distant lowing, feeling that the exaltation of their souls

95

was shared by the whole of nature. When they got back to the house Clara picked a jasmine flower and gave it to him. Gauna kept that jasmine until a short time ago.

XXVI

Girls should be blonde, statuesque, like those figures of the Republic or of Liberty, golden-skinned and with grey or at least blue eyes. Clara was slim and dark with that prominent forehead he hated. From the beginning, he loved her. He forgot the adventure of the lakes, he forgot the boys and the Doctor, he forgot football. As for the races, a certain bond of gratitude made him follow the fortunes of Meteoric from Saturday to Monday for a few weeks – fortunes moreover which proved as fleeting as the enigmatic brilliance to which the horse owed its name. He did not lose his job because Lambruschini was good-natured and tolerant, and he did not lose Larsen's friendship because friendship is a noble and humble Cinderella, used to privations. With great patience and a good deal of humiliation and skill, he devoted himself to the task of making Clara fall in love with him and of making himself disliked by almost everyone he had to deal with. At the beginning Clara had made him suffer, treating him with a frankness that was perhaps worse than lies. This was not deliberately perverse: she had undoubtedly been candid and loyal as always. Everything gets known in the end and Larsen and the boys wondered why Gauna put up with so much. Clara was a girl with a certain prestige in the neighbourhood at that time – an important fact that her later image, companionable and submissive, tends to make us forget – and perhaps, as some people thought, there was as much vanity as true feeling in that passion of Gauna's. We cannot know for certain today; and as, after

97

all, that cynical and malicious doubt could equally well be raised in the case of all other love affairs, it is perhaps more important to bear in mind the explanation that Gauna gave Larsen one evening: 'I made her fall in love with me so that I could forget her.' (Larsen, always so ready to believe his friend, thought he was not speaking the truth on that occasion.) After that inexplicable folly with Baumgarten, the girl fell in love with Gauna and, as people said, became sensible. She withdrew from her friends in the Eleo company, taking part only in the single performance of *The Lady from the Sea*, said to have been a triumphant success – a performance from which Gauna, paralysed by pride though pricked by jealousy, stayed away – and she did not see her friends again. The Turkish girl said that after the trip to the country Clara loved Gauna with a real passion.

Between work and Clara, Gauna's days passed rapidly. In their world, as secret as the tunnels of an abandoned mine, lovers perceive differences and subtleties in hours when nothing happens except declarations of love and mutual compliments; but in fact, walking arm in arm in the early evening between seven and eight is much like walking arm in arm between seven and eight any other evening, and strolling in parque Saavedra on Sunday and going to the cinema from five to eight is much like strolling in parque Saavedra another Sunday and going to the cinema from five to eight. All those days, so similar to one another, passed rapidly.

About this time Gauna told Larsen and other friends that he would like to go and work on a ship or help with the harvest at Santa Fe or in the Pampas. Now and again he toyed with these imaginary flights, but then he would forget them and even deny having planned them. Gauna wondered whether a man could be in love with a woman and yet desire with a desperate and secret determination to be free of her. If he imagined any accident happening to Clara – her suffering or falling ill for any reason – his hard boyish indifference vanished and he wanted to cry. If he imagined her giving him up or loving someone else, he felt physically ill and was filled with hatred. He was endlessly skilful in devising ways to see her and be with her.

XXVII

It was Sunday afternoon. Gauna was alone in the room, stretched out on the bed, smoking, with his bare feet up, in slippers, crossed in the air. Clara had stayed at home to be with her father Don Serafín, who 'was in a poor state of health'. Gauna was to go and see them at seven.

They had decided to get married. They had reached the decision involuntarily and inevitably, without either of them suggesting it.

Larsen came back. He had gone to the baker's to get the cakes for the maté.

'I could only get little buns.' He unwrapped the packages and showed the contents to Gauna, who barely looked. 'I propose we set up as bakers.'

Not without envy Gauna reflected that his friend lived in a simple world. He went on to think that Larsen was in fact very straightforward but that there was a certain stubbornness in his character. They couldn't talk about the girl – or at least they couldn't talk about her easily. Before the trip to the country it was because Larsen mistrusted her and because he clearly disapproved of the passion that had turned Gauna's and Clara's life into a secret and, at the same time, a public spectacle (he disapproved both of that passion and of all passion); and after the trip it was because, having got to know Clara, he would have condemned any disloyalty on Gauna's part. To Larsen, Gauna's desires to run away seemed incomprehensible. Perhaps he felt a friendship and respect for Clara that Gauna himself was incapable of feeling for any woman.

Perhaps there were subtleties Gauna was unable to understand in the simplicity of his friend.

He reflected that if they couldn't talk about that subject, it wasn't only Larsen's fault. More than once Larsen had begun to speak to him but he, Gauna, had always changed the subject. Any talk about the girl irritated and almost offended him. He had become quite friendly with Ferrari and the two of them would discuss emphatically, with illustrations, what a disaster women were. Of course, in Gauna's mind these vituperations against women in general were really directed specifically against Clara. And so he felt no need to talk about her.

'If you're not chained to the bed, you lazy creature,' Larsen teased his friend affectionately as he took the maté pot out of the cupboard, 'perhaps you could toast one of these buns a little.'

Gauna did not reply. He was thinking that if anyone had raised the idea of marriage it certainly hadn't been Clara or Clara's father. 'I have to admit,' he said to himself, 'that the idea probably came from me.' Perhaps once when he was with Clara, acting on an impulse of tenderness, he had wanted, in a confused way, to get married, and had immediately proposed marriage there and then, in order to refuse her nothing, to keep back nothing for himself. But now he couldn't tell. When he was with her he was so different from when he was alone ... When he was with her the thoughts he had had when he was alone seemed false, and annoyed him as though someone were attributing alien feelings to him. Now that he was alone he thought he ought not to marry. Soon, though, when he saw her again, his unvarying future in Lambruschini's garage and worse still in his own home wouldn't matter, wouldn't even exist. His one wish would be to prolong the moment they were together.

Gauna got up, took a tin fork with all its teeth bent out of the cupboard, speared a bun and held it up to the flame of the heater.

'You see,' he said, spearing a second bun, 'if I had toasted them earlier they'd be cold by now.'

'You're right,' said Larsen, passing him the maté.

'What will you do?' Gauna spoke with difficulty and with sadness. 'What will you do when I leave? Will you stay here or move?'

'But why are you going?' asked Larsen, surprised.

'The wedding,' Gauna reminded him.

'Of course,' said Larsen. 'I hadn't thought of it.'

Gauna felt a sudden burst of annoyance with Clara. Through his own fault something in his life was dying and, what was worse, something in Larsen's too. They had lived together for many years and it was a pleasant and peaceful routine for both of them; it seemed wrong that one of them should break it.

'I shall stay here,' said Larsen, still perplexed. 'Although it's a bit expensive I'd rather stay in this room than go and look for another.'

'I'd do the same if I were you,' agreed Gauna. Larsen brewed more maté. Then he said quickly:

'How stupid I am. Perhaps the two of you would like this room yourselves? I hadn't thought of that.'

The words 'the two of you' increased Gauna's animosity towards the girl. 'No, I wouldn't take this room from you under any circumstances. In any case it would be too small for us.' The word 'us' also rankled with him. He went on: 'I'm going to miss my bachelor life. Women clip your wings, if you see what I mean. With their trivial concerns they make you prudent and half-feminist, as the German in the gymnasium used to say. In a few years' time I'll be more domesticated than the baker's cat.'

'Stop talking rubbish,' Larsen's words were heartfelt. 'Clara isn't just pretty. She's exceedingly pretty and worth more than you and I, the baker and the cat. Tell me something, why don't you stop making such a fuss?'

XXVIII

As Gauna was getting ready to go out that same evening, just as it was beginning to get dark, there was a downpour of rain. He waited in the entrance hall for it to stop, and he noticed how all the usual colours of the neighbourhood – the green of the trees, lighter in the case of the eucalyptus whose leaves were quivering beyond the waste ground in the distance, darker in the case of the paradise trees on the pavements, the browns and greys of the doors and windows, the white of the houses, the ochre of the draper's on the corner, the red of the posters still vainly announcing the sale of plots of land, the blue of the glass sign opposite – all these had taken on the boundless intensity of living things, as if some frenzied exaltation had reached them from the depths of the earth. Gauna, normally rather unobservant, was struck by this and made a mental note that he must tell Clara about it. Strange how a women we love can enlarge our understanding – for a while.

A lot of water had collected in the streets and at some corners people were using temporary bridges to cross. In avenida del Tejar he met Pegoraro, who, after touching him as though to convince himself that Gauna was not a ghost, slapped him on the back and embraced him, exclaiming: 'Where on earth have you been hiding?'

Gauna muttered something and tried to continue on his way. Pegoraro went with him.

'It's ages since you've shown your face at the club,' he remarked, stopping a minute, opening his arms wide and exposing his palms.

'Yes, it is,' admitted Gauna.

He wondered how he could get rid of Pegoraro before arriving at the Sorcerer's house. He did not want him to know that was where he was going.

'If you could see the new team now, you'd think you were back in the good old days. You'd have to admit that there's nothing in the world like football. The club's unrecognizable. We've never had a forward line like this, I swear by my own mother, who gave me this little medal. Ever seen Potenzone?'

'No.'

'Then don't talk about football. You'll just have to keep quiet; in other words, shut up. Potenzone's the new centre-forward. A wizard with the ball, full of flourishes and finesse, but when he's in front of the goal, loses all his impetus, no sticking power, and messes up even the easiest goal, see what I mean? And Perrone? Haven't seen him either?'

'No.'

'But what on earth are you up to? You're missing the best moments in life. Perrone is the fastest wing we've ever had. An altogether different case. Runs like an arrow, gets all set for a goal but then loses his head and shoots outside. And Negrone – seen him?'

'In my time he was almost a veteran.'

While Pegoraro, turning a deaf ear, began expounding on Negrone's faults, Gauna thought that one of these Sundays he'd have to invent some good excuse and go back to the club. Nostalgically he remembered the time when he never missed a single match.

Pegoraro asked him:

'And where are you off to now?'

Gauna thought that the girl would be waiting for him in front of the entrance and realized it did not bother him if Pegoraro knew where he was going. He remembered what Larsen had said about Clara and smiled with satisfaction.

'To Taboada's house,' he replied.

Pegoraro stopped and opened his arms again, showing

104

his palms. With his head on one side, he asked:

'You know, that man really is a sorcerer. Remember the afternoon when we went to see him? Right. Remember how my legs were covered with boils? Right, well the bloke muttered some words under his breath – I couldn't even catch them – then he seemed to be making some scribbles in mid-air, and the very next day – not a single boil. I swear it on that medal. I didn't let on to anyone, I can tell you. Didn't want them to think I'd been taken in by witches' spells.'

Clara was waiting for him in the entrance. From a distance she did not look particularly pretty. He remembered how at the beginning, when they used to meet in the street or in other public places, he took pleasure in imagining the envious approval with which people saw him take her by the arm. Now he was not even sure she was pretty. He said goodbye to Pegoraro, who asked him:

'So when are we going to see you over at the Club?'

'Soon, Fatso. I promise you.'

Until Pegoraro was out of sight, Gauna did not cross the street. The girl rushed up to greet him and gave him a kiss. She shut the door, then turned on the light and they got into the lift.

'What do you think of this rain?' asked Clara, as they were going up.

'Very heavy.'

He remembered his intention of talking to her about the violence of the colours and of the light after the downpour, but he suddenly felt annoyed and said nothing. They went into the little hall.

'What's the matter?' asked Clara.

'Nothing.'

'What do you mean – nothing? Come on, tell me what's the matter.'

Gauna had to find some explanation. He asked:

'Are you still seeing Baumgarten?'

To conceal his hesitation, he spoke very loudly. Clara made signs that people could hear what they were saying. The delay in replying maddened him.

'Answer me,' he insisted angrily.

'I never see him,' Clara assured him.

'But you think about him.'

'No, never.'

'No? Why did you go out with him that evening?'

He cornered her against the divan and pestered her with questions. Clara did not look at him.

'Why? Why?' he insisted.

Clara looked him straight in the eyes.

'You were driving me mad,' she said.

Slightly hesitantly, Gauna asked:

'And now?'

'No, not now.'

She was silent, calm and smiling. Gauna placed her on the divan and leant back beside her. He thought: 'She's a little animal, a poor little animal.' He kissed her tenderly. He thought: 'Close to she *is* pretty.' He kissed her on the forehead, the eyelids and the mouth. After a while he said:

'Let's go and see your father.'

Clara remained lying there and did not open her eyes. Finally she got up very slowly and went over to a mirror, looked at herself with a vague smile on her lips, exclaimed: 'What a face!' and shook her head. She tidied herself up a bit, smoothed down a lock of Gauna's hair, put his tie straight, took him by the hand and knocked on the door of her father's room.

The Sorcerer was in bed and he had on a shirt that was wide open at the chest and so big that it seemed to make him look particularly small and thin by comparison. His long grey hair fell behind in a noble disorder, leaving his high narrow forehead clear. The whiteness of the sheets was impeccable.

'What do you think of this rain?' he asked, stubbing out a cigarette in the ashtray on the bedside table.

'Very heavy,' acknowledged Gauna.

The room displayed a mixture of carelessness and pretension, an unattractive and impoverished hetero-geneity, doubtless due to the lack of any sense of style, and a bareness, not total but forbidding – qualities not at all characteristic of Argentine houses, inside or outside,

106

whether in town or country. Taboada had a narrow iron bed painted white, and the bedside table, also white, was made of wood and very simple. There were three Viennese chairs and against a wall a small sofa with an arm at one end, covered in cretonne (when Clara was four or five years old it had been upholstered in horsehair); on a corner table you could make out the telephone nestling inside a rag-doll in the form of a Negress (there are similar ones made like hens to be used as tea-cosies); on top of a modern, cedarwood chest of drawers, with black, shiny handles, there was a flower that was pink when the weather was fine and blue when it was going to rain, a box made of shells and mother-of-pearl with the inscription 'Souvenir from Mar del Plata', a photograph in a beaded velvet frame of Taboada's parents (of an earlier period, certainly less refined than Taboada but much more so than the ancestors of all his neighbours) and a copy of the book *Sham Geniuses in the Struggle for Life* by José Ingenieros, in an embossed leather binding.

'All that,' explained Taboada, noticing the curiosity with which Gauna was looking at the objects on top of the chest of drawers, 'was given to me by Clara. The poor thing's going to spoil me with all these presents.'

The girl left the room.

'How are you feeling today, Don Serafín?' asked Gauna.

'Not bad,' replied Taboada. Then he added, smiling, 'But this time Clara got a fright. She won't allow me to get up.'

'What do you expect? You must rest. Let other people do the work, while you have a smoke and read the paper, stretched out on the sofa.'

'On my bed of pain, you mean. But it's nothing serious. Do you know what she did?' asked Taboada, laughing. 'That girl is going to ruin me. But don't tell anyone. She brought along a doctor and forced me to see him.'

Gauna looked at him intently and spoke seriously. 'You should look after yourself. What did the doctor say?'

'When he was alone with me, he told me I shouldn't spend the winter in Buenos Aires. But not a word of that

107

to Clarita. I don't want anyone meddling and making decisions for me.'

'And what have you decided?'

'To take no notice of him, to stay in Buenos Aires where I've spent all my life and not go wandering, like a loaf that won't sell, over the hills of Córdoba, learning to speak in their sing-song way.'

'But Don Serafín,' insisted Gauna obsequiously, 'if it's a question of health...'

'Come on. Don't be a nuisance. I have changed, or I believe I have changed, the destinies of others. Let mine follow its course, whatever that may be.'

Gauna could not insist because Clara had come back. She was carrying a tray and served them coffee. They talked about the wedding.

'I shall have to invite Dr Valerga and the boys,' hinted Gauna.

As always, Taboada retorted: 'Doctor of what, may I ask? Of the art of frightening the young and the weak.'

'As you like,' replied Gauna, without getting annoyed, 'but I shall have to invite him.'

Taboada spoke to him very gently:

'Emilito, the best thing you can do is to break with all that crowd.'

'When I'm with you I feel like you, but they're my friends.'

'One can't always be loyal. Our past usually makes us ashamed, and one can't be loyal to the past at the cost of being disloyal to the present. I mean that there's no greater disaster than a man who doesn't follow his own judgement.'

Gauna did not reply. He felt that there was some truth in Taboada's words and above all that Taboada would find plenty of arguments to reduce him to silence if he tried to discuss the matter. But he was nevertheless convinced that loyalty was one of the most important virtues and, thinking back on the confused words he had just heard, he even suspected Taboada held the same view.

'What always put me off marriage is the hubbub,'

confessed Taboada, as if thinking aloud.

'We could get married without inviting anyone or having a reception,' suggested Clara.

'I thought for girls the main thing was the wedding dress,' said Gauna.

Taboada lit another cigarette. His daughter removed it from his mouth and stubbed it out in the ashtray.

'You've smoked enough for today,'

'You see how bossy she is,' said Taboada calmly.

Gauna looked at his watch and got up.

'Aren't you going to join us for lunch, Emilio?' asked the Sorcerer. Gauna told him that Larsen was waiting and said goodbye.

'I wanted to ask you both a favour,' said Taboada, arranging the pillow so that he could sit up better in bed. 'When you next go for a walk, go as far as calle Guayra and have a look at my little house. It's small and unpretentious but I would think it would do for working people. It's my wedding present to you.'

When he was alone Gauna reflected that for Clara to leave her father would be more painful than for him to leave Larsen. Sorcerer and all, Taboada seemed to him worthy of compassion, and Gauna felt it was very cruel to be taking his daughter away from him. Clara must feel that too, though she had never mentioned it. Gauna wondered incredulously whether she felt the same resentment towards him that he felt towards her.

XXIX

They were so busy settling in that the significance of the marriage itself – a ceremony at which the witnesses were Don Serafín Taboada and Don Pedro Larsen – was somehow forgotten by the protagonists and got mixed up with the other chores and worries of a very hectic day. Taboada and Larsen did not share this indifference.

As he had promised, Taboada made them a present of the house in calle Guayra, which was his only possession. Gauna took over the mortgage, on which there were only a few payments outstanding. Gauna and Clara told him they could not accept such a huge present, but Taboada assured them that the income from his consultations was ample for his modest lifestyle.

Despite the fact that they had not sent out any invitations, they received presents from Lambruschini, from Gauna's workmates at the garage, from the Turkish girl and from Larsen. The latter must have almost bankrupted himself because he presented them with a dining-room suite. Blastein, director of the Eleo Company, sent them a white metal cocktail-shaker, which Gauna lost in the move. The whole neighbourhood knew they had got married, but the discreet manner in which they had done it provoked a certain amount of malicious comment.

Gauna asked for time off from the garage and for a fortnight Clara and he worked hard at home. Gauna was so absorbed that he never gave a thought to the problem of his lost liberty; mortgages, the arranging of the furniture, whitewashing, carpeting, putting up shelves, fixing boilers, seeing to the electricity and gas took all his attention. With particular care he built a little bookcase for Clara, who was a great reader.

In the bedroom they put a double bed. When he suggested buying a folding-bed in case one of them should be ill, Clara replied that there was no reason for them to fall ill.

Gauna went to the Platense Club very rarely and only so that they would not think he was annoyed with them or looked down on them or that Clara held him prisoner. The first evening they met in Valerga's house Antúnez asked, to embarrass him:

'Do you all know that our young friend here has taken the vows of matrimony?'

'And may one ask who is the fortunate young lady?' asked the Doctor.

Gauna thought his ignorance must be feigned and felt he was in an awkward situation.

'The Sorcerer's daughter,' Pegoraro informed him.

'I don't know the girl,' declared the Doctor seriously, 'but I do know the father. He's a fine man.'

Gauna looked at Valerga with almost pious affection, remembering the contempt with which Taboada invariably spoke of him. At the same time, with increasing alarm, he began to wonder whether Taboada's disdain might not be justified. He went on talking in order to banish these thoughts.

'It was a private wedding,' he said by way of explanation.

'As though they were ashamed,' commented Antúnez.

'That seems an unfounded observation,' said the Doctor, looking menacingly at Antúnez.

'There are those who like the hilarity of celebrations and those who don't. I got married like Gauna, with no striped awnings or idiots gawking.' He looked searchingly at all those around him. 'Any objections?'

Gauna hardly remembered the adventure of the lakes, but one night when he could not sleep, he thought of that mystery again and with an absurd feeling of exaltation he vowed to solve it one day, and then vowed not to forget

111

his resolution. He was sure that if he went back and saw the sunrise in the wood at Palermo, the place itself would reveal something to him. He must also question Santiago again; to think that perhaps El Mudo knew the truth! He would have to go round the cafés and if necessary pluck up courage and appear in the Armenonville in hired evening dress. Perhaps some dancer, if he bought her a drink, would tell him what she had seen or what she had been told.

That same night he also remembered his plan to fight Baumgarten. He knew that a chance combination of circumstances had delayed and finally prevented the fight; but he also knew that if people had known the truth of the matter, they would have considered him a coward. And he wasn't sure that that judgement would have been wrong.

XXX

As money was short during those years, it became quite
difficult to pay the mortgage and they had to do without
some things. Nevertheless, they were happy. Gauna went
straight home as soon as he left the garage; on Saturdays
they had a siesta and then went to the cinema; on Sundays
Lambruschini and his wife would take them in the Lancia
to Santa Catalina or El Tigre. The four of them also went
to motor races on the track at San Martín, and the ladies
pretended to be interested. Once they got as far as La
Plata, and wandered absent-mindedly round the Natural
History Museum. When they got home, in a volume
called *The Treasures of Youth*, lent to them by a man who
was a dentist, they discovered and were terrified to see
pictures of prehistoric monsters which they imagined had
been drawn from life. In summer, together with Larsen,
they went swimming on the beach at La Balandra and,
with the rhythmic ebb and flow of the river before them,
they talked of distant lands and imaginary journeys. They
also talked of a feasible journey: a return visit to Chorén
beside the Las Flores river; but that project was never
realized. Clara and Gauna did not give up hope of saving
enough to buy a Model T Ford and go out by themselves.

Some afternoons Gauna would go to the Sorcerer's
house when he left the garage. Clara would be waiting for
him there, and Larsen too. Sometimes when he saw them
there, he felt that the three of them made a family group
and that he was an outsider. He immediately felt ashamed
of the thought.

One afternoon they spoke about courage. With astonishment and not without protest, Gauna heard them say that according to Taboada, he was braver than Larsen. The latter seemed to accept the statement as an indisputable fact. Gauna said that his friend was always ready to face anyone in a fight and that he, that he, that he ..., he was going to add something, a truthful and candid admission, but they would not listen to him. Taboada explained: 'The courage Gauna is talking about is unimportant. What a man must have is a kind of philosophic generosity, a certain fatalism that enables him to be always ready, like a man of honour, to lose everything at that moment.'

Gauna listened to him with admiration and incredulity.

At that time – 'to broaden their horizons' – Taboada was teaching them a little algebra, a little astronomy and a little botany. Clara studied too; her intelligence was perhaps more intuitive than that of Gauna and Larsen.

'How surprised the boys would be,' exclaimed Gauna one day, 'if they knew I was spending the evening studying a rose.'

Taboada commented: 'Your destiny has changed: two years ago you were on the way to becoming another Dr Valerga. Clara saved you.'

'Partly Clara,' Gauna admitted, 'and partly you.'

At the beginning of the winter of 1929 Lambruschini suggested that he become a partner in the firm, and Gauna accepted. It seemed a good time to make money: nobody was buying new cars, and the old ones were falling to bits; as Ferrari reckoned, 'everything on four wheels will end up in the garage'. But the crisis was so bad that people preferred to abandon their cars rather than take them to the garage. None of that endangered their happiness.

He had been told that people who live together start feeling contempt for each other, and then irritation. He felt an infinite need of Clara – of knowing her, of getting close to her. The more he was with her, the more he loved her. When he remembered his old fears of losing his freedom he felt ashamed; they seemed naïve and contemptible quibbles.

114

XXXI

It was a Sunday in winter, at siesta time. Lying in bed, covered in blankets, stretched out amidst a chaos of picture sections from the papers, Gauna was gazing absent-mindedly at the delicate play of shadows reflected on the ceiling. He was alone in the house. Clara, who had gone to see her father, would be back at five, in time to go to the cinema. Before leaving, she had advised him to go out and have a walk in the sun in the plaza Juan Bautista Alberdi. So far, his only sortie had been to the kitchen to heat water for maté. Back in bed again, he stretched out an arm, rapidly brewed the maté, took two or three gulps, bit off the crust of a French loaf (Larsen had told him that drinking maté without eating anything gave you a stomach-ache), left the maté and bread on a chair that served as a bedside table, and wrapped himself up again. He thought that if he could reach his hat – it was on a wicker table near the door – without getting up, he would put it on. But the brim, he told himself, would irritate the nape of his neck. The older generation were right. Abandoning the nightcap was downright unfair to the head. He felt sorry for his ears and nose and just as he was thinking of putting on ear and nose protectors someone knocked at the door.

Gauna got up grumbling; shivering with cold, treading on the edges of the blanket he was wrapped in, he made his way to the door as best he could, and opened it.

'Well, you take your time, don't you?' It was the woman who cooked for the carpenter. 'Phone call for you.'

115

Immediately she was gone, grey and small like a rat. Very alarmed, Gauna tidied himself up a bit and, still only half-dressed, hurried round to the carpenter's. In a strange voice Clara told him that her father was not very well.

'I'll come straight over,' said Gauna.

'No, that's not necessary,' Clara assured him. 'It's nothing to worry about. Only I'd rather not leave him by himself.'

She told him to go out and get a change of scene. He spent all the week stuck in that freezing garage; he needed to relax; he had been looking very thin and worried lately; had he been for a walk in the square to get some sunshine? Before Gauna could tell a lie, she suggested that he should go to the cinema for them both. Gauna said 'yes' to everything. Clara went on, saying that he should come and collect her at about eight and they could have any old thing for supper; maybe they could open one of those tins they could never decide to try.

Gauna thanked the carpenter (who did not reply or even look up) and went back to his house. He realized that the opportunity he had desired for so long had arrived. That very afternoon he would undertake a fresh investigation of the adventure of the lakes, of the mystery of the third night. He felt neither the slightest impatience nor hesitation. It pleased him to think that the decision which had been, as it were, hovering round him within reach, waiting for the opportune moment, was now taken. A superficial observer might have thought him weak-willed, with no pressing urge to clear up this particular mystery. Well, it was not like that. Now that the chance had come, he would prove it.

His plan, it is true, was so vague that it would have been absurd to say to Clara one Saturday or Sunday: 'We won't go out together today.' Or go out by himself in the evening and put God knows what ideas into her head. And if, after all, she had actually forced him to explain himself (for women can be very insistent), he would have sounded like a liar or an idiot.

He took the maté things to the kitchen and was on the

116

point of throwing the used leaves into the sink when he paused, poured some hot water on to them and drank. It was disgusting; he spat it out, finished washing the things and put them back in the cupboard.

Though he had on a woollen shirt, he put on the cardigan Clara had knitted him (he had always been openly hostile to cardigans, and the colour of this one, in particular, seemed too bright and gaudy to be worn by a man, but poor Clara got upset if he disdained the present, and today, what the hell, the cold was really ferocious). He covered himself up as well as he could; if he did not put on an overcoat, it was because the moment to buy one had never come.

He walked briskly to keep out the cold, but when he got to Saavedra station he felt tired and listless. He bought a ticket to Palermo, and sat down to wait for the train. But no sooner had he done so than he realized that he had no really well-thought-out plan at all. What would he do when he got to Palermo but wander round the woods like some poor fool? Where would that lead? Nowhere. Much better to plan it properly in advance. For the moment, he would go to a film with Larsen. He was embarrassed by the ticket in his pocket. Could he just hand it back? No, the ticket-clerk was a complete stranger. He got up and walked out of the station. If Larsen were not at home, he decided, he would make use of the ticket after all. But why should Larsen not be at home?

When he got near his old haunts he was always assailed by a certain nostalgia, perhaps a feeling of tenderness and perhaps of bad temper. Absent-mindedly he went into the house and reached the door of his old room. He knocked. There was no reply. The landlady – whom he first shouted for, and whom he then offended, by his impatient indifference to her well-meant greetings and enquiries – told him that Señor Larsen had just gone out, and shut the door in his face. Back in the street, Gauna hesitated for a second. Should he go back to the station, or present himself at Taboada's? At that moment El Musel appeared, pedalling his light-blue tricycle, a great big

117

smile on his hairy face. El Musel was an employee of *La Superiora*. (It was not his real name, but everyone called him that because of his habit of bringing the name of his birthplace into every conversation.) Gauna asked him if he knew where Larsen had gone.

'No, I don't know, I really don't,' El Musel replied. 'Well, and how about you? What's this, wandering round on your own? Tired of married life already? Impossible. Quite impossible.'

They slapped each other amicably on the back and Gauna went on his way towards the station. He regretted having put that question to El Musel. 'And besides,' he thought, 'how can I let slip the chance to begin the definitive investigation?' No matter how much he tried to hide it from himself, he was worried and nervous. He got to the station in time to jump into the last carriage just as the train was pulling out. He got out at avenida Vértiz, went under the bridges, crossed the Rosedal and went into the wood.

XXXII

He was very cold. The wind whistled through the bare trees, and the ground, covered with a mass of dead leaves and branches, felt soggy underfoot. Gauna was expecting, or hoping for, a sudden revelation. He wanted to concentrate on that third night. But his mind switched to the thought that his shoes were getting wet and that there were some people, Larsen for example, who as soon as they got their feet wet could sense a sore throat on the way: 'a pressure on the throat' was how he described it. Gauna swallowed, and was aware of a slight soreness. 'My thoughts are straying,' he told himself, 'I must concentrate.' Without thinking he had approached a car and he now noticed that a couple inside it were watching him suspiciously. He walked off as if he had not seen them. After wandering about a little longer, shivering with cold, acutely conscious of everything he was doing and of the fact that he must be looking either very shady or very stupid, he decided to give up the investigation for that afternoon. He would go back past the house on the landing-stage. Perhaps he would find Santiago there; perhaps a few words from him would be more useful than roaming all afternoon in these desolate woods. Perhaps Santiago and El Mudo had learned how to behave properly and now offered their visitors a glass of brandy, which, as Pegoraro was in the habit of saying, always warms you up and makes a meeting more friendly and interesting.

When he got to the house on the lake, Santiago and El

Mudo were drinking maté. It struck Gauna that he was not having much luck that afternoon, but he resigned himself to the maté, which, to make matters worse, was offered with the accompaniment of little biscuits covered with milk chocolate. (El Mudo took them out of a huge blue tin, into which he plunged his hand, as into a lucky dip.) He began to enjoy the combination of the bitter maté and the biscuits, which he had not liked at first, and very soon, instead of a feeling of cold which had made his spine shiver, he felt a warm and subtle sense of well-being invade him. They talked, like brothers, of the years when Gauna had played in the fifth division and Santiago and El Mudo had been caretakers. Santiago asked if it was true, as he had been told, that he had got married, and congratulated him. Gauna told them:

'You may not believe this, but there are times when I still wonder what really happened the night El Mudo found me in the wood.'

'You were bothered with suspicions right from the start,' explained Santiago, 'and now it's no good – no one will get these ideas out of your head.'

Gauna was surprised; the way strangers see one is always surprising. But he did not object; he understood vaguely but clearly enough that the true explanation could not for the moment be given. If he were to declare: 'I am not trying to discover anything evil. I am trying to discover the supreme moment of my life, in order to understand it', Santiago would look at him with distrust and resentment and wonder why Gauna was trying to deceive him. Santiago went on:

'If I were you, I'd forget the whole stupid business and make up your mind to lead a quiet life. Besides, I don't know what to say to you. If you can't worm the truth out of your friends, I don't see how you're going to discover it.'

Hypocritically, Gauna continued:

'And what if I'm mistaken? I can't let them see I'm suspicious of them.' He looked at Santiago in silence; then he added: 'You haven't managed to find out anything more about the circumstances in which El Mudo found me, have you?'

'Anything more, my friend? It's an old story now and nobody thinks about it any longer. Besides, who's going to get anything out of El Mudo? Look at him, he's more tightly shut than a safe.'

El Mudo could not have been as tightly shut as his brother said, because he began to make noises with his throat, short and anguished. Then, silently, he laughed so much that the tears ran down his cheeks.

'And can you remember the place they snatched you away from, to come to the wood?' asked Santiago.

'From the Armenonville itself,' Gauna replied.

'Pick up one of the dancers, question her closely, taking your time over it, and who knows? Maybe you'll discover something.'

'I've thought of that, but look at me, just look at me. How can I go to the Armenonville in this shabby outfit? I'm not going through all the rigmarole of hiring a suit, and the doorman won't let me in like this, unless I were to wait on the doorstep till the next carnival.'

Santiago looked at him seriously and, a moment later, speaking slowly, he asked:

'You know what the drinks will cost you? At the very least five pesos – I tell you at the very least. You sit yourself down and before you open your mouth they're pouring out champagne; and as soon as some girl approaches you can put your fingers in your ears because they'll be uncorking a second bottle, because the brand you had does not please the young lady, who is very particular in her tastes. And while you're lolling back comfortably don't forget that they've put a taximeter in your wallet and when you want to throw in the sponge and leave, more dead than alive, be sure you hand out tips because if the waiters are dissatisfied they'll shove you out and they'll hand you over to the doorman who'll beat you up and you'll wake up in the police station and be fined for disorderly conduct.'

They had finished their maté. El Mudo, always unpretentious, was replacing the leather on an oar. Santiago, smoking a pipe and dressed in a vast blue jersey, walking up and down on his landing-stage, looked like an old sea-dog. They said goodbye.

'Well, Emilio,' said Santiago warmly. 'Don't you disappear for good this time.'

XXXIII

Gauna walked across the gardens, and skirting the zoo, reached plaza Italia. As the cold forced him to walk quickly, he got tired. He waited a while for the No 38 tram; when at last it appeared, it was full of people coming back from the races. He clambered on to the back platform, his arms tired and his body stiff with cold. He reached the centre of town and got off at the corner of Leandro Alem and Corrientes. He told himself he would have a look at the little cafés (he meant to say the 'cabarets') of calle 25 Mayo.

On the third night of the carnival of 1927, before going into the Cosmopolita Theatre, they had had a drink in one of those cabarets. He wanted to find it again now, but he was so cold and tired that he did not spend very long looking for it. In fact, he went into the first establishment he came to. It was called Signor. Its entrance hall was long and narrow and painted red, with flames and devils all over the walls no doubt to represent the way to hell, or at least to some infernal pit. There were also coloured photographs; some showed women with castanets, wearing capes, twisted into wild, animated postures; others showed dancers in top hat and tails; and there was one of a little dimpled girl, winking with a provocative smile on her face. When he got inside, two women were dancing a tango that was being picked out with one finger by another woman at a piano. A fourth was sitting at a table, looking on, leaning on her elbows. Two men were working, up behind the bar. Some of the tables were laid, others had chairs upside down on them.

Gauna gave the door a push to go out.

'Want something, governor?' said one of the men.

'I thought you were open,' explained Gauna.

'Well, sit down,' said the dishwasher, 'it's a bit early, but we won't throw you out. What can I get you?'

Gauna gave him his hat and sat down.

'Double brandy, please.'

Maybe this was where he had been that night. Surreptitiously, he stole a glance at the women; one of those dancing looked like an Indian from La Pampa and the other (as he told Larsen later) 'had the face of an idiot'. The one at the piano was very small with a big head. The one sitting down was a blonde with a face like a sheep. She got up unwillingly; Gauna said to himself, not without apprehension, 'she's coming over'; the woman approached him, asked if she were disturbing him, and sat down at his table. When the waiter approached, the woman asked Gauna:

'Will you buy me a soda-water?'

Gauna said that he would. The woman ordered:

'With plenty of whisky, please.'

To cover up his anxiety Gauna remarked:

'I don't like cold tea myself.'

The woman explained about the medicinal virtues of whisky, assured him that she was actually drinking it on doctor's orders and 'believe me, because I like it', and she launched into lengthy descriptions of the illnesses she'd been plagued with, mainly of the stomach and intestine, that had ended in her losing a lot of weight, and that now Dr Reinafe Puyó, whom she had met one morning by pure chance, was treating her with whisky and other beverages less agreeable to the palate, which left her all churned up, lying like a poor invalid on her bed with a handkerchief soaked in eau-de-cologne on her belly. Gauna was impressed. He admitted to himself (though it was shameful to confess it) that he had not had a lot of experience with women, and that if he found himself with a girl, who was not one of the dolls of the neighbourhood, he was a little intimidated and helpless, without much willpower. Their glasses were refilled and Gauna thought: 'I know this woman's face.' (Perhaps he thought he knew it because it was the type of face, with variations and peculiarities, that one often comes across.) After Gauna had drunk his third double brandy, the woman revealed that she was called 'Baby' (she pronounced the name with a broad 'a') and he plucked up courage and asked if they hadn't met in the same place during a carnival, two or three years ago.

'I was with some friends,' he explained. After a pause, with a change of tone, he added: 'You must remember. A middle-aged man was with us, rather fat and respectable-looking.'

'I don't know what you're talking about,' replied Baby, visibly agitated.

Gauna insisted: 'But you must remember.'

'I must, must I? That's enough. Who are you to come and upset me, just when the doctor's told me that getting worked up is the very worst thing for me?'

'Take it easy,' said Gauna, smiling. 'I'm not trying to sell you anything and I'm not a policeman on the track of a murder. Apart from which, I don't want you to get upset.'

The woman's irritation seemed to abate. If he got the chance, he would have to come here again; perhaps with time he would manage to get some information; Baby was no idiot, one had to admit.

When she spoke again, he could detect in her voice a note of reassurance and almost of acceptance:

'Promise me you'll be nice and not bring up anything nasty?'

Gauna looked at his watch and called the waiter over. It was already eight o'clock; he wouldn't get to the Sorcerer's house before nine. The woman asked:

'You're leaving me.'

'I'm afraid I have to,' replied Gauna and, forestalling any protest, he half-shut his eyes, pointed a finger at her, half-reinforcing a point, half-accusing, and added with a note of conviction: 'I've seen this little face somewhere before.'

125

'Now you're getting boring again,' Baby told him, smiling.

She had understood Gauna's tactics and had got the joke, but she preferred not to detain him.

Gauna paid without protest, said to Baby 'Goodbye beautiful', quickly collected his hat and left. He ran down calle Lavalle. Then he took the tram. Despite the cold, he preferred to stay on the back platform (the inside of the tram, like that of churches, was for women, children and old people). The conductor looked at him, seemed about to say something to him but then changed his mind and went up to other people:

'Pass along inside, please.'

Gauna was annoyed. 'What a way to waste the afternoon,' he said to himself. By the English Clock Tower he saw that it was half-past eight. Who could tell what might have happened to Taboada, and here was he roaming round the wood till late and then chatting up one of those silly women with faces like sheep. In a moment, when he arrived, what would he say to Clara? That he'd gone out with Larsen. Tomorrow morning early he'd go to Larsen's house to warn him. But what if Clara had been with Larsen? He wiped his forehead with his handkerchief and murmured: 'What a bore the whole thing is.' The conductor, standing beside him, was listening to a man who was considering the merits of one of the horses that had run at Palermo that afternoon. The conductor then said to the man:

'But do you know who you're talking to, my friend? I saw Monserga race at Maroñas!'

'That's ancient history, old man,' said the man. 'The world's moved on since then. Everything moves on. Yet here you are, Alvarez, still dreaming about those prehistoric horses – compared with the horses we've got today, they moved like tortoises.'

'Listen to him! He's so sure of himself! Look, when you were still sucking a dummy I was studying the form and putting my money on Serio, who always used to lose to Rico. And tell me, who was the Golden Cup champion? Mind you, the track was nothing but mud. And if I asked you who Don Padilla was, what would you say? Come on then!'

Gauna thought that perhaps he would find Larsen at Taboada's. How could he find out whether they had gone out that afternoon? If he were to discover something, they would never see him again. 'My God,' he murmured, 'how can I even imagine such a thing?' He covered his eyes with his hand. He got off the 38 in calle Monroe, caught the 35, and when he got to avenida del Tejar, it was almost half-past nine. He wondered whether it wasn't too late; whether Clara wouldn't be waiting for him in calle Guayra. He looked up and saw that the light was on in Taboada's apartment.

XXXIV

At the door he bumped into a man who greeted him. In the lift there were three people whom he did not know. One of them asked him:

'Which floor?'

'Fourth.'

The man pressed the button. When they got out there, he opened the door for Gauna to get out. Gauna got out, but then saw to his surprise that the others were following him. Confused, he murmured:

'You too?'

The door was half-open; the men went in; there were people inside. Then Clara appeared; dressed in black – where had she got that dress from? – her eyes shining, she ran and threw herself into his arms.

'My darling, my love,' she cried.

Pressed against him, he could feel her trembling. He wanted to look at her but she hugged him more tightly. 'She's crying,' he said to himself. Clara told him:

'Papa is dead.'

Then, in front of the kitchen sink, where Clara was sponging her eyes with cold water, he heard for the first time the story of the last hours and death of Serafín Taboada.

'I can't believe it,' he repeated, 'I just can't believe it.'

The previous evening Taboada had been seized by coughing fits and shortness of breath, but he had said nothing. Today, when Clara had rung Gauna, Taboada was listening, and it was on her father's instruction that she had asked him to go to the cinema. 'You ought to go too,' he added; 'but I won't insist, because I know you won't take any notice. There's nothing to be done here, and unhappy memories should be avoided.' Clara protested; she asked him if he wanted her to leave him alone. Taboada replied very gently: 'One always dies alone, Clarita.'

Then he said he was going to rest a little and shut his eyes. Clara was not sure if he was sleeping. She would have liked to ring Gauna, but would have had to use another telephone and did not dare to leave her father. A moment later he asked her to come over to him. He stroked her hair, and with a voice now very weak, said to her: 'Take care of Emilio. I interrupted his destiny. Try to prevent him from resuming it. Try to stop him becoming a gangster like Valerga.' He sighed and went on: 'I should like to explain to him that there is generosity in happiness and selfishness in adventure.' He kissed her on the forehead and added in a murmur: 'If you like, Clarita, you can ring Emilio and Larsen now.' Concealing her emotion, Clara rushed to the telephone. The carpenter at the other end was bad-tempered; she thought she had been cut off, but he eventually said that there was no reply and that Gauna must have gone out. Then she rang Larsen. He promised to come at once. When she went back to the bed she saw that her father's head had dropped gently down on to his chest and she realized he was dead. He had obviously asked her to make the telephone calls so that she would not be there at the actual moment of death. He had always said that one had to take great care where memories were concerned because one's life was made up of them.

Clara went into her father's bedroom. Gauna, uncertain, remained in the kitchen, looking at the sink, strangely aware of the presence of the objects around him, observing himself in the act of looking at them. He had not moved when Clara came back in to ask him if he'd like a cup of coffee.

'No, no,' he said, feeling ashamed. 'Is there something I should be doing?'

'No, nothing, darling,' she replied, calming him.

He realized it was absurd that she should be comforting him, but he felt she was so superior to himself that he did not protest. Suddenly he remembered something and said with a start:

'But ... the funeral ... Should I go and make arrangements for it?'

Clara replied:

'Larsen's already taken care of it. I also sent him home to see if you were there and to fetch some things.' Smiling, she added: 'Poor thing, look at this dress he brought over.'

Though she was not much of a coquette, she found something absurd in that dress, something that he did not notice.

'It looks very good on you,' he said, and then he added: 'There are lots of people.'

'Yes, there are,' she agreed. 'Could you go and look after them?'

'Of course, of course I will,' he replied quickly.

As soon as he left the kitchen, he found himself among strangers, who embraced him. He was moved, but he realized that the news of this death had come too abruptly for him to know how much it affected him. When he saw Larsen he was very moved.

The people were drinking coffee, which Clara had served them. Gauna sat down in an armchair. He was surrounded by a group of men; they were all talking in low voices; suddenly he heard himself say:

'It was suicide.'

It gave him pleasure to note the interest the statement provoked; he hated himself for that feeling.

'It was suicide,' he repeated. 'He knew he couldn't survive another winter in Buenos Aires.'

'Then he died like a great man,' declared 'cultured' Señor Gómez, who lived on lottery tickets. He was very thin, very grey and very pale; his hair was cut close and his moustache was sparse. His eyes were small, wrinkled, ironic, and, as people put it, Japanese; he was dressed in a dark suit with a shawl over his shoulders; when he moved and even when he talked he trembled from head to foot. What was most striking about his appearance was his extraordinary frailty. In his youth, it was said in the neighbourhood, he had been a formidable trade unionist, and, worse still, a Catalan anarchist. Now, thanks to his impressive collection of matchboxes, he had allied himself with the best families. Gauna thought: 'There's nothing like funeral wakes for hearing idiotic remarks.'

'If you think about it,' Gómez went on, 'Socrates' death was no more than suicide. And that of ... And that of ...'

('He's forgotten the second example,' Gauna said to himself.)

'And even that of Julius Caesar. And that of Joan of Arc. And that of Solís, who was eaten by the Indians.'

'Evaristo is right,' pronounced the pharmacist.

Gauna calmed down. The Pole from the shop, with his light-blue eyes, drowsy look and appearance of a fat cat curled up asleep inside a house, explained:

'What worries me is the staircase ... very narrow ... I don't see how they're going to get the catafalque out.'

'The coffin, you bloody idiot,' corrected the pharmacist.

'Ah yes, that's it,' continued the Pole, 'the first thing I look at in houses is the width of the staircase ... I don't see how they're going to get it out.'

A very well-dressed young man, whom Gauna observed with suspicion, wondering whether he wasn't one of those who go to wakes for the coffee, declared vehemently:

'What is really monstrous, at a time like this, is the neighbours on the third floor. They're playing music, knowing there's a wake going on just above their heads. They make me want to go and present a formal complaint to the porter.'

Above Señor Gómez's shawl, which was dotted with dandruff, Gauna saw that someone was greeting Clara. 'Who can that big-head be?' he thought. He was pale and blond; Gauna thought he recognized him from some-where. 'They seem to know each other. I must ask Clara who he is. Not now though. It would be a bit awkward to ask her now,' he said to himself. 'But I must ask her who he is.'

Fragile Señor Gómez went on:

'We hold on to life tenaciously, with all our claws. You can tell a great man when he takes leave of life like Taboada, without a futile struggle, with a rapid and almost joyous decision.'

On the pretext of greeting them, Gauna approached the group of women. The blond boy left. Lambruschini's wife was very affectionate. Gauna thought: 'The Turkish girl improves every day, but as for Ferrari's fiancée, she's fearsome.' The conversation and the coffee helped to pass the night. In a corner, some people played *truco*, but they were frowned upon by the rest.

XXXV

The concept of destiny is a useful invention of man. What would have happened if certain events had been different? What happened is what had to happen – a modest lesson that shines with a humble but diaphanous light in the story I am now telling you. Nevertheless, I still believe that the fate of Gauna and Clara would have been different if the Sorcerer had not died. Gauna began to go again to the Platense Club and to see the boys and the Doctor. The neighbourhood gossips said Gauna saw to it that these brief absences from home did not upset his wife by arranging that Larsen should take his place, and that when one went out the other went in ... In fact it was all quite innocent. Larsen's feelings for Gauna and Clara never changed; he could no longer go to the Sorcerer's house so he went to Gauna's.

Without the guidance of the Sorcerer, Gauna talked about the adventure of the three days almost all the time. Clara loved him so much that in order not to be excluded from anything concerning him, or simply in order to imitate him, she also began discussing the subject when she was alone with the Turkish girl. She must have sensed that Gauna's obsession concealed an abyss in which her happiness would finally be dashed to pieces; but she possessed that noble resignation and fine courage that some women have, managing to be happy in the lulls between sorrows. In fact not even these lulls were free from a shadow, the shadow of an unfulfilled desire, to have a child (apart from Gauna, only the

Turkish girl knew of this).

Gauna began to speak more and more openly about his memories of the carnival, the mystery of the third night, and his vague schemes to unravel it. It is true that he was more guarded when Larsen was present, but he went so far as to mention the masked girl at the Armenonville in front of Clara. If he earned a few pesos in the garage, instead of saving them up for the Ford or the sewing-machine or the mortgage, he spent them running around bars and other establishments where he and his friends had gone during those three nights in 1927. At times he realized the uselessness of these sorties: the same places, when seen separately, without the exhaustion, the drink and the madness of that first occasion, aroused no memories in him. Larsen, whose prudence seemed in the end like cowardice, brooded too much over Gauna's escapades and let the girl sense his worry. One afternoon, speaking with veiled anger, Clara told Larsen she was sure Gauna would never abandon her for another woman. Clara was right, though a blonde with a strangely sheep-like face, who worked as an entertainer in a seedy bar, the Signor, in the southern part of town did captivate him for almost a week. At least that was the rumour that went round the neighbourhood. Gauna talked very little of the matter.

When Gauna inherited Toboada's money – some 8,000 pesos – Larsen was afraid he would squander it on three or four wild chaotic nights; but Clara never doubted Gauna. He paid off the mortgage and brought home the sewing-machine, a radio and the few pesos left over.

'I've got you this radio,' he told Clara, 'so that you'll have something to entertain you when you're alone.'

'Are you thinking of leaving me alone?' asked Clara.

Gauna replied that he couldn't imagine life without her.

'Why didn't you buy the car?' she asked. 'We wanted it so much.'

'We'll get it in September,' he promised, 'when the cold spell is over and we can go for outings again.'

It was a rainy afternoon. Her forehead pressed against the window-pane, Clara said: 'How lovely to be together, hearing the rain outside.'

She served him some maté. They talked about the third night of the carnival of 1927. Gauna said: 'I was at a table with a masked girl.'

'And then what happened?'

'Then we danced. I heard a clash of cymbals, the dancing stopped, everyone joined hands and we began running round the room in a chain. Then the cymbals clashed again and we paired up again but with different partners. And so I lost the masked girl. As soon as I could I went back to the table. The Doctor and the boys were waiting for me to pay their bill. The Doctor suggested we go for a walk around the lakes to cool ourselves down a bit so we wouldn't end up in the police station.'

'What did you do?'

'I went out with them.'

She didn't seem to believe him.

'Are you sure?' she asked.

'How could I not be sure?'

'Are you sure you didn't go back to the table where the masked girl was?' she insisted.

'I'm certain, my love,' replied Gauna, kissing her on the forehead. 'You once said something to me that no one else would have said. It upset me at the time but I've always been grateful to you for it. Now it's my turn to speak frankly. I was in despair about losing that masked girl. I suddenly saw her leaning against the bar; and I was going to get up and go over to her when I realized she was smiling at a fair-haired boy with a big head. I was infuriated, perhaps precisely because of my happiness at seeing her. Or perhaps it was jealousy. Who knows? I don't understand anything. I love you, and it seems impossible to me that I could have felt jealous because of someone else.'

As if she had not heard him, Clara went on: 'What happened after that?'

'I agreed to take a walk around the lakes, got up, left the money we owed on the table and went out with Valerga and the boys. Then there was a quarrel. I can see it as in a dream. Antúnez or someone else said I'd won

135

more on the races than I'd let on. At that point everything becomes crazy and confused, as things do in dreams. I must have made a terrible mistake. As far as I remember, the Doctor sided with Antúnez and we ended up fighting with knives in the moonlight.'

XXXVI

On the morning of Saturday, the 1st of March 1930, Gauna was comfortably installed in the barber's in calle Conde.

'So you haven't got any tips for this afternoon's races, Pracánico?' he asked the barber.

'Don't talk to me about races,' replied Pracánico. 'I don't want to end up in the loony-bin. Betting is a mug's game. Not roulette, of course. I always lose my shirt on roulette at Mar del Plata; nor am I talking about the lottery, which swallows up my holiday money every week – the money I'm saving in the hope of going to Mar del Plata in the summer.'

'What kind of a barber do you call yourself?' said Gauna. 'In the old days barbers always gave racing tips. And they kept you amused, a different story for each customer, exactly tailored to his sense of humour.'

'If that's what you want, I'll tell you my life story,' said Pracánico. 'It's as good as a novel. I can tell you about my time on a battleship, when I was so scared I didn't have time to feel seasick. Or the time I went out with the greengrocer's wife. Her husband was in Rosario, so I took my chance.'

Gauna hummed:

> *I sing the Canguela,*
> *And I lead a life of woe,*
> *For my beloved girl,*
> *That I dream of every day,*
> *Has left here for Rosario,*
> *Rosario de Santa Fe.*

'I didn't catch that,' said Pracánico.

'It's nothing. Just a song I remembered. Go on.'

'Well, I seized the opportunity. I went out with the greengrocer's wife that night. I was young in those days and had quite a few fans.' Looking round and raising his eyes in genuine admiration, he added:

'I was tall.'

(He did not explain how he could possibly have been much taller than he was now.)

'We went to a dance, a really swish affair, at the Teatro Argentino. I was unbeatable at the tango. Well, as we were dancing the first dance, this thug with a hoarse voice cut in and said, "My turn now, boys. I'm the King of Córdoba." I guess the fool thought it was one of those dances where you change partners in the middle. But I didn't argue. I just said he could have her and that I was tired of dancing anyway, and I made a bee-line out of the theatre. I didn't want to cross swords with a character like that. But next day the woman came round to the shop that I had at calle Uspallata around the 900s, and told me never to make such a miserable spectacle of myself at the dance again. Another time we were having a siesta cuddled together, and some little disagreement blew up. Would you believe it, I saw her get up, open a chest and take out a great Solingen knife! All she was going to do was cut a slice of bread and dulce but bread and dulce was the last thing I was thinking of. I yelled that I caved in, and went down on my knees like a saint and with tears in my eyes implored her not to kill me!'

As Gauna was looking at him in some surprise, Pracánico explained with great vehemence, and even with a certain pride: 'I'm no good in situations like that. I don't mind swearing on anything you like that I'm a wretched coward. It was the same when I started going out with Dorita. She'd only just split up with her husband. One night when I was on my way to see her, I suddenly came up against her husband blocking the way in a nasty dark spot. He said: "I want a word with you." "With me?" I said. "Yes, with you," he said. I said: "There must be some mistake." "No mistake at all," he said: "You'd better arm yourself double quick, because I'm armed." I began shaking like a leaf. I swore a thousand times that it was all a mistake, and I explained that there was no shop that sold knives in the neighbourhood and anyway it was after closing. And I begged him to let me ring my daughters and say goodbye to them, and after that he could do whatever he liked with me. By that time he must have realized that he was dealing with a gibbering idiot, a contemptible cretin. His anger faded away. He became perfectly reasonable and told me to go and see Dorita and then come and have a talk with him in a café. I'd have liked to pretend that I didn't know who Dorita was, but I just didn't have the nerve, if you see what I mean. When I got to Dorita she asked me what the matter was. I said I'd never felt better in my life. But you know what women are like: she kept saying that I looked like someone who'd been scared out of his wits. When I left her, her husband was waiting for me and we went to a café, since that was his whim. I made him a sincere offer of friendship, but for some reason he kept making difficulties. Finally he came out with it – he worked in the naval dockyard. Could I wangle him a bit of promotion? Well, I gave in at once. I swore there and then that I'd get it for him and the next day I began pestering my relations. I did it so well that by the end of the week it was all settled, his promotion was signed and sealed. After that we became great friends and used to meet every evening. Sometimes all three of us would go out to the theatre together, quite respectably, like a family. Five years went by like that, with us seeing each other every day. In the end the poor man died of an abscess, and I could breathe again.'

As he was putting his tie back on, Gauna reverted to his first question: 'So you really don't have any tip for the races?'

A gentleman dressed in black, carrying an umbrella and with a face like a bird of ill omen, who had been quietly waiting his turn for some time, now got very agitated and said:

'Say yes, Pracánico, say yes. I've got an absolute winner.'

Pracánico irritably took the money that Gauna handed him. Gauna looked in his jacket pocket and found an old tram ticket to write on. He took out a pencil and looked at the man in black. In a weak, hissing voice, screwing up his mouth in an effort to be as distinct as possible, the man enunciated – and Gauna wrote down in capital letters – the name: CALCEDONIA.

XXXVII

And as some of you may remember, on that 1st of March, Calcedonia won the fourth race. When Gauna called at the barber's towards the end of the day, he received from the hands of Pracánico 1,740 pesos. At the café on the corner they celebrated their victory with corked vermouth and slightly over-ripe cheese.

Gauna knew that he ought to have been happy, but he made his way home without any feeling of elation. By awarding him this piece of good luck, destiny, which usually governs our lives subtly and unseen, had thrown off its disguise and revealed itself with a directness that was almost brutal. For Gauna took it to mean one thing: he had to spend the money as he had done in 1927; he had to go out with the Doctor and the boys; he had to go to the same places, get to the Armenonville on the third night and be in the wood at dawn. In this way he would be able to perceive again the visions that he had known that night and then lost, would grasp firmly and finally what had been for him, as in the ecstasy of a vanished dream, the culmination of his whole life.

He could not say to Clara: 'I've won this money on the races and I'm going to blow it with the boys and the Doctor during the three nights of the carnival.' He could not announce that he would squander that money stupidly – money that was badly needed in the house – with the additional provocation of three nights of alcohol and women. He might be able to do it; but he could not admit it. He had already got used to hiding certain thoughts

141

from his wife; but to be with her that evening and not to tell her that the following evening he would be going out with his friends seemed to him a treacherous concealment, and furthermore, impracticable.

Clara greeted him tenderly. The trusting joy of her love was reflected in her whole person; in the brilliance of her eyes, in the curve of her cheeks, in her hair carelessly brushed back. Gauna felt a kind of spasm of pity and of sadness. It was monstrous to treat someone who loved him so much like this. And after all, for what reason? Were they unhappy together? Would he rather have had any other woman? As though the matter was out of his hands and was going to be decided by a third person, he found himself wondering what would happen the following day. Then he resolved that he would not go out; that he would not abandon (the mere thought of the word made him shudder) Clara.

It was late when they turned out the light. I think they even danced that night. But Gauna did not tell her that he had won on the races.

XXXVIII

Sunday dawned cloudy and rainy. Lambruschini invited them to go to Santa Catalina.

'It's not a day for excursions,' declared Clara. 'Better stay at home. Later on, if we feel like it, we can go to the cinema.'

'As you like,' Gauna said.

They thanked Lambruschini for the invitation and promised to go out the following Sunday.

They spent the morning doing very little. Gauna read the *History of the Girondins*; between the pages he found the slip of paper with its red inscription: 'Freyre 3721' written by Clara in lipstick, the evening of their first date. Clara cooked lunch, which they ate, and then they had a siesta. When they got up Clara said:

'I don't really want to go out today.'

Gauna began working on the radio. The evening before he had noticed that the coil began over-heating after it had been on a while. Around six o'clock he announced:

'There, I've fixed it.'

He took his hat and put it far back on his head.

'I'm off for a little walk,' he said.

'Will you be long?' asked Clara.

He kissed her on the forehead.

'I don't think so,' he replied.

He told himself that he didn't know. Earlier, when he had asked himself what he would do that evening, he had felt a certain anguish. He no longer felt that. Now, secretly at peace, he could observe both his indecision,

143

which was perhaps real, and his freedom, which was perhaps illusory.

'It hasn't rained enough,' he thought as he crossed plaza Juan Bautista Alberdi. The trees seemed enveloped in a halo of mist. It was very hot.

The boys were sitting round a marble table at the Platense, feeling bored. Pale and preoccupied, Gauna leant over the backs of the chairs where Larsen and Maidana were sitting, and said:

'I've won more than a thousand pesos on the races.'

He watched their reaction. Looking back on it later, but not at the time – he was too tensed up – he thought he had noticed an expression of anxiety on Larsen's face. He went on:

'I want to invite you out this evening.'

Larsen indicated 'no' with his head. Gauna pretended not to notice. He went on talking rapidly:

'We must enjoy ourselves as we did in '27. Let's go and get the Doctor.'

Antúnez and Maidana got up.

'Have you got fleas?' asked Pegoraro, leaning back in his chair. 'You see, my friend, they're behaving just like the brutes they are. Are we going to leave here without celebrating Emilito's luck, even if it's only with Bilz? Sit down, if you please. We've got plenty of time. There's no need to hurry.'

'How much did you win?' asked Antúnez.

'More than 1,500 pesos,' answered Gauna.

'If you ask him in a moment,' insisted Maidana, 'it'll have gone up to over 2,000.'

'Waiter!' called Pegoraro. 'This gentleman here is standing us a round of rum.'

The waiter looked enquiringly at Gauna, who nodded.

'Rum for everybody,' he said. 'It's on me.'

At the end of that round they all got up, except Larsen. Gauna asked him: 'Aren't you coming?'

'No, old man. I'm staying.'

'What's the matter with you?' asked Maidana.

'I can't go,' replied Larsen, with a knowing smile.

'Let her wait,' advised Pegoraro. 'It's good for them.'

144

Antúnez remarked:

'He believes it.'

'If not, why wouldn't I be coming?' asked Larsen.

Gauna said to him:

'But you'll join us tonight, won't you?'

'No, Emilio. I can't,' said Larsen.

Gauna shrugged his shoulders and began to move off with the boys. But he went back to the table and said in a low voice to his friend:

'If you can, drop by the house and tell Clara I've gone out!'

'You should tell her that yourself,' replied Larsen.

Gauna caught up with the group.

'So who's Larsen going to meet?'asked Maidana.

'No idea,' replied Gauna curtly.

'Nobody,' said Antúnez. 'Can't you see it was just an excuse?'

'An excuse pure and simple,' repeated Pegoraro sadly. 'That boy is lacking in human warmth, he's selfish, he just wants a quiet life.'

Antúnez intoned in his honeyed voice, of which even his friends were by now weary:

> *In a contest with destiny*
> *No one can win.*

XXXIX

'How much did you win?' asked the Doctor. His thin lips sketched a subtle smile. 'It's always been my opinion that there is no nobler sport.'

He was wearing a workman's blue jacket, dark patterned trousers, and sandals. He had received them coldly but the news of Gauna's triumph had softened him considerably.

'One thousand, seven hundred and forty pesos,' replied Gauna with pride.

Winking an eye and hunched on his left leg, Antúnez remarked with enthusiasm.

'That's what he's declared so far. If you like, I'll look inside his pants for you!'

'Please don't use those coarse expressions,' said the Doctor severely. 'I shall make a point of reprimanding you every time you start talking like a young thug. Decency, boys, decency. That crazy Almeyra, who was never far away whenever any particularly blatant crime was being carried out or extravagant folly committed – not to mention the notoriety he acquired when it was the fashion among the *jeunesse dorée* to chase policemen – this man told me (I shall never forget it) that being respectably dressed paid off more handsomely than gambling at cards.' Then resuming his friendly tone, he said: 'But why don't you come in?'

They went into the kitchen and, sitting on crudely made benches and rush-seated chairs (one of them very low indeed) they formed a group round the Doctor. Solemnly

146

he brewed maté, drank some and offered it round.

At last Gauna found the courage to speak:

'We were thinking of going out and having a good time during the carnival. We should like you to honour us with your company.'

'I've already told you, my boy,' replied Valerga, 'that I'm not a circus; I have no company. But I accept the invitation with pleasure.'

'When the Doctor finds out when the invitation is for, he'll shoot little Gauna,' remarked Antúnez, with a nervous giggle.

'When is it for?' asked the Doctor.

'Today,' Gauna replied.

The Doctor turned to Antúnez:

'What did you think, eh? Think I'm past it, do you? Too set in my ways to do anything on the spur of the moment?'

In order, perhaps, to head off this discussion, Maidana asked: 'Where shall we go?'

Gauna realized he had to appear decisive.

'We shall follow the 1927 circuit again,' he said.

'The same places?' said Pegoraro in alarm. 'Why? We've got to see what's new, we've got to keep up with the times.'

'And who are you to have an opinion on the matter?' asked the Doctor. 'It's Emilio's choice, because it is he who won the money. Is that clear to everyone, or do I have to shout it into their ears? I hereby give my consent to anything he cares to propose, even if he wants to walk round and round the same places like an animal tethered to a wheel.'

The Doctor went through to the room next door, and came back a few seconds later wearing a handkerchief round his neck, his vicuña scarf, the dark jacket, the same trousers and very shiny patent-leather shoes. Preceding and surrounding him was an almost feminine aura of the scent of carnation or, perhaps, of talcum powder. His hair was freshly combed and shone with grease.

'Troops, quick march,' he ordered, opening the door for the boys to leave. He turned to Gauna: 'What now?'

'First we must go to Pracánico the barber's,' said Gauna. 'My win is entirely owing to him. It would be very mean not to invite him along too.'

'He always wants to go around with barbers,' remarked Pegoraro.

'Perhaps he doesn't remember the saying,' suggested the Doctor: 'Go to the barber's and you come home without even a wig.'

They all laughed a great deal at this. Pegoraro whispered in Gauna's ear. 'He's in a very good mood' – his voice expressed admiration and affection – 'I don't think we need worry about any unpleasant scenes for the time being.'

They had to knock at the barber's door for quite a while, and the Doctor had begun showing signs of impatience when a woman appeared.

'Is Pracánico here?' asked Gauna.

''Course he isn't. How could he be?' said the woman. 'You know very well how he works himself to death all the year, always in the front line, slaving away and doing his duty; well, you can hardly imagine how he lets himself go at carnival time. Savastano – that's another one I can't stand – came from the plaza del Once to fetch him, and the two of them have gone off together, hoping to get a place on Doctor Carbone's allegorical float.'

At Saavedra station they took the train. Gauna realized that his plan of repeating exactly the actions and route of the three days of the 1927 carnival was impracticable. The absence – or as he could not help putting it to himself, the desertion – of the barber, hurt him. He consoled himself by the reflection that even if he had managed to get Pracánico, the group would not have been the same, since on the strictest analysis, Pracánico was not Massantonio. But they were both barbers, and that was surely the crucial factor. The original group in 1927 had consisted of the Doctor, the boys and a barber. The sad truth was that they were now setting out on their circuit without a barber.

XL

They got out at Villa Devoto and went along Fernández Enciso to plaza Arenales. On the way they met some masked people who seemed ashamed and lost. Maidana murmured:

'Just as well they're not squirting water at us.'

'If they so much as splash me,' remarked Antúnez darkly, 'I'll get out my 38 and give them an extra eye in their heads.'

The Doctor tapped Gauna on the shoulder.

'Your little expedition may turn out to be rather a flop,' he said, smiling. 'The animation of previous years is conspicuous by its absence.'

'Do you remember the carnival of 1927?' asked Gauna. 'The avenues seemed like one huge parade.'

'It's not even eight o'clock,' observed Maidana, 'and everybody seems to be falling asleep. There's no life, no animation. It's hopeless.'

'It's hopeless,' agreed the Doctor. 'In this country everything's going wrong, even carnivals. There's only decadence.' After a few seconds he added slowly: 'The darkest decadence.'

'Let's go and have a drink in that club with the Brazilian name, Los Mininos or something like that,' suggested Gauna.

Maidana shook his head, after which he deigned to explain:

'They won't let us in; we're not members.'

'We went in the other time,' insisted Gauna.

'The other time,' Pegoraro informed them, 'El Gomina had friends there.'

Maidana silently indicated his agreement. They walked on a while, not bothering, perhaps, in what direction.

'It's too early to feel tired,' protested the Doctor. They went on walking. Then they noticed a carriage.

'There goes a victoria,' shouted Gauna.

They hailed it. Valerga ordered the driver:

'To Rivadavia.'

The Doctor and Gauna sat on the main seat; the three boys behind. Maidana, who had sat down a little to one side and practically outside the carriage, asked:

'Haven't you got a shoehorn, Governor?'

The Doctor replied upon reflection:

'We must look for a café where they give you a decent meal. I could do with a grill.'

'I'm not hungry,' Pegoraro volunteered sadly. 'I'll just have a slice of salami and a few little meat pies.'

It struck Gauna that the outing in 1927 had been very different, right from the first evening. As though he were talking to the boys, he said to himself: 'There was a different feeling of animation then, a different sense of human solidarity.' It seemed to him that he himself had been less preoccupied with his personal situation on that occasion; he had given himself in a more carefree fashion to the group of friends and the animation of the evening. Perhaps in 1927 they had already had two or three drinks when they left Saavedra. Or perhaps he thought he was now remembering the initial moments of the other outing but was in fact remembering later moments, the end of the first evening or halfway through the second.

'Perhaps I'd do better to have some Spanish stew,' continued Pegoraro, after some reflection. 'With this weight I've got on my stomach, I'd better stick to light meals.'

Gauna had by now become convinced that the state of mind of 1927 was irrecoverable. But even so, when they broke away from a parade and went down a little, deserted, twisted street, he did think he could sense it again, as one senses a forgotten melody, in snatches, distant, recurrent and faint.

'Be so kind, Doctor, as to take a look at the chicken,' exclaimed Pegoraro, leaning half out of the carriage. They were turning back into an avenue and had almost grazed the kerb. 'That chicken, Doctor, the second one along on the spit ... behind you ... now out of sight. Don't tell me you didn't see it.'

'Forget it,' the Doctor advised him. 'You go in, tuck your napkin under your chin, and find yourself getting plucked cleaner than the bird.'

'Don't insult Gauna,' begged Pegoraro plaintively.

'I'm not insulting anyone,' replied the Doctor sternly.

Alarmed, Maidana intervened.

'What Pegoraro meant is that today Emilito isn't going to bother about a few miserable pesos.'

'Why do you say I'm insulting him?' persisted the Doctor.

Antúnez winked and curled up on the seat. Jokingly, he explained:

'We must take care of Gauna's little stash of money as if it were ours.'

'We're not going to find another chicken like that,' moaned Pegoraro.

'Stop, Governor,' Valerga ordered the driver, with a shrug; to Gauna he said: 'Pay, Emilito.'

As they went into the restaurant, the Doctor explained:

'In my day chicken was for women, invalids and foreigners. We men ate grilled meat, if I remember correctly.'

A small, sweaty old man, with a dirty jacket, a greasy napkin under his arm, very wrinkled and drooping trousers, with a yellow glint probably due to ironing burns, came and gave the table a cursory wipe. Valerga said to him:

'Listen, young man; this gentleman here' – he pointed to Pegoraro – 'has got his eye on one of those chickens that are turning on the spit in the window. He'll show you which one.'

When they came back with the chicken, the waiter asked:

'Would you like anything else?'

'We'll see,' said Pegoraro. 'Why don't you bring us the menu?'

Doctor Valerga shook his head.

'In my day,' he said, 'no one went hungry, though we weren't constantly asking for the bill or the menu. We'd sit up at the counter, give the waiter a fixed sum to cover the meal, and we weren't surprised if he served up three dozen fried eggs.'

'I've been working in this country for forty years,' declared the waiter, 'and may I be struck blind if I have seen such a thing. Perhaps the gentleman read about it in some collection of old wives' tales.'

'Are you calling me a liar?' demanded the Doctor, 'or do you want me to kill you?'

Maidana intervened diplomatically:

'Don't take any notice of him, Doctor. He's just an old man who doesn't know what he's saying.'

'Don't worry,' replied Valerga. 'I'm as meek as a lamb. I'm not going to bother with this old creature. As far as I'm concerned, let him serve us and then let the worms devour him.'

'But Doctor,' implored Pegoraro, 'this little chicken isn't going to be enough for all of us.'

'Whoever said it should be? The boys'll begin with a plate of cold meat; Gauna and I, who are the respectable ones here, will see to the chicken, and you, being delicate, will have some bread soup and a vegetable or two.'

Gauna pretended not to notice the Doctor winking at him. By now he was fed up with his jokes and his nasty temper. Taboada had been right. Valerga was an unbearable old man. He was ruled by a spirit of dogged, vulgar spite. As for the boys, they were just poor devils, budding delinquents. Why had it taken him so long to realize this? To go out with this bunch of idiots he had left the house, without telling his wife where he was going. Would Clara still love him? Without her and Larsen he would be absolutely alone.

He pushed his plate aside. He was not hungry. The Doctor was finishing off half a chicken, the boys were wolfing and fighting over slices of mortadella and salami. Pegoraro was gulping down his soup. Gauna looked at them with loathing.

'Not eating?' Pegoraro asked him.

'No,' he replied.

Pegoraro promptly seized the portion of chicken Gauna had left and began devouring it. The Doctor looked annoyed but said nothing. Gauna took a swig of wine. Then, as he waited for the Doctor and the boys to finish their meal, he drank three or four glasses. The Doctor suggested they go and visit one of the establishments in calle Médanos.

'The one with the German girls, remember? We patronized it in 1927.'

XLI

As they felt very full, they decided to walk. They finally reached calle Médanos. The establishment was closed. Almost all the places they had gone to in 1927 were now closed. They came out into an avenue, and while their ears were assaulted by a band of musicians playing non-stop, the Doctor related how, years before, he had set fire to a masked girl who had snubbed him.

'You should have seen how the poor thing raced along, with her raffia costume and guitar they called a ukulele. In the crime section of the papers they called her "the human torch".'

In a café, now near Rivadavia, Gauna remembered that they had been there in 1927, perhaps at the very same table, and that something had happened concerning a boy. For a second he thought he could remember the episode and feel what he had felt that night. He asked:

'I think there was some story with a little boy here. Can anyone remember what happened?'

'I remember absolutely nothing,' declared the Doctor.

'Strike me dead if I remember anything at all,' said Antúnez.

Gauna thought that if only he could recall that episode he would have the key to those marvellous, lost experiences ... but the state of mind he had enjoyed in 1927 now seemed totally irrecoverable. Today he was not abandoning himself to a warm feeling of brotherly love, a feeling of almost magical power, a feeling of carefree generosity. Today he was a watchful and hostile onlooker.

154

After drinking a small glass of gin, Gauna glimpsed one detail of the carnival of 1927. Feeling very shrewd, he asked:

'Where shall we spend the night, Doctor?'

'Don't worry,' Valerga replied. 'A doss-house is easy to come by in Buenos Aires.'

'It's my opinion,' said Pegoraro, 'that Emilito is ready for bed. He seems down in the dumps, and hasn't got much energy.'

Gauna went on:

'Last time we went to a farm belonging to a friend of the Doctor.'

'To a what?' asked the latter.

'A farm. A bad-tempered woman with a lot of dogs came out to greet us.'

Valerga merely smiled.

The boys talked freely, as though they realized the Doctor was not in the mood for telling them off.

'So you want to economize now, do you?' demanded Pegoraro. 'A man in your position hasn't got to look after every wretched peso.'

Antúnez intervened with a certain warmth.

'Don't take any notice of him,' he said. 'My motto is that we shouldn't make you spend one centavo more than you have to.'

'They don't understand you, Emilito,' said the Doctor, speaking almost gently. Then, turning to the boys, he explained: 'For some reason known only to himself, Emilito wants us to repeat what we did in 1927. It must be that no one needs to know the reason, or surely he would have told us, his friends.'

'But, Doctor –,' protested Gauna.

'I do not like to be interrupted. I was saying that we are your lifelong friends and that I am surprised to find you keeping things from us. I would never have forgiven anyone else for doing this. The mere thought of it makes my blood boil. But with Emilito it's different; he's the man who is lucky, who has had the courtesy to think of us and make us his guests and, in a word, no one can say I do not know how to be grateful.'

155

'But, Doctor, I assure you ...,' insisted Gauna.

'You don't need to justify yourself,' interrupted the Doctor, resuming his friendly tone. Then he turned to the boys: 'There are times when we want to return to the places we frequented in the golden days of our youth. There are such times, I say, because not even the most manly of men can free himself from the memory of a certain woman.' He turned back to Gauna. 'I want to tell you that I approve of your conduct. You are right not to talk about it. The small men of today reveal everything and have no thought for the reputation of the lost woman who listened to them.'

Gauna wondered whether he ought to believe the Doctor, and whether he ought to believe that the Doctor believed what he had said. Did he believe it himself? Wasn't the real purpose of this pilgrimage to commemorate his previous meeting with the masked girl at the Armenonville? Or was he repeating the pilgrimage in the magical hope that the encounter itself might be repeated?

They had another round of gin and then left the café. The Doctor announced in a tone that gave nothing away:

'Now we're going to the farm.'

Antúnez nudged Maidana. They both began laughing; so did Pegoraro. But Valerga frowned at them so severely that they quickly smothered their laughter.

They could hear the noise and see the lights of Rivadavia from quite a distance. They passed a group of two young girls, dressed as *manolas** and a young man in pirate's costume.

'Whew!' exclaimed the young man. 'Lucky we got out of there.'

'The parade was odious this year,' commented one of the girls. 'You couldn't take a single step without some disgusting creature...'

'Did you notice that one,' the other girl interrupted, 'I really thought he was going to eat me up with his eyes.'

'And with that heat I swear I thought I was going to be suffocated,' said the young man.

---

*in local costume

'Really,' murmured Valerga.

Pedlars were wandering around offering veils, false noses, masks, streamers and boxes of brilliantine-tube water-squirts; surreptitiously, local boys were offering – cheap – tubes of brilliantine already used, but refilled (with water from the gutter, so it was said). Other pedlars were offering fruit, fresh or crystallized, Laponia ices, ring-shaped rolls made of cornflour, cakes and peanuts. They made their way through the crowd, to look at the parade. While they were contemplating the capers of some little angels on an allegorical float, a red-headed girl succeeded, from a vast, hired double-phaeton, in flinging a little red ball right in the Doctor's eye. Visibly enraged, the Doctor made as if to hurl a water-squirt at her that he had snatched in the heat of the moment from a tearful little boy dressed up as a gaucho, but Gauna managed to restrain him. After that incident, the boys and the Doctor advanced slowly through the crowd, staring at girls and shouting aggressively at them, and stopping at cafés for glasses of rum and gin. Then, in a taxi, they followed the interminable throng, handing out compliments and insults on their way. When they reached the point where street numbers were in the 7,200s Valerga ordered:

'Stop, driver. I can't take any more.'

Gauna paid. They went into another café, and after a while turned down a small tree-lined side-road going southwards, probably calle Lafuente. Their drunken shouts echoed in the silence of the deserted neighbourhood.

To the left, detached against a sky of moonlit clouds, stretched the long pale walls and high chimneys of a factory. Suddenly, instead of walls, Gauna saw steep ravines with tufts of grass on top of them, some pines and a few crosses. The air was heavy with the sweet suffocating smell of smoke. There were no more lights; one last solitary street-lamp shone out over the ravines. They went on walking. Big clouds had hidden the moon. Now, to the left, he thought he could make out a dark plain; to the right, undulating ground. Round lights came and went on the plain to the left. Out of the depths of the darkness, a

157

pair of these lights was advancing rapidly. Suddenly Gauna saw the head of a horse, enormous, almost on top of him. Perhaps because of the profusion of monstrous masks he had seen that evening, the peaceful head of the animal frightened him as though it were something diabolical. He understood; to the left was a ranch; the round lights were the horse's eyes. Then his legs gave way, and he thought he was going to faint. He remembered something and then dizzily forgot it, as one remembers and forgets a dream on waking up. When he was able to recapture that memory, he expressed it in the question:

'What happened on that same evening, in 1927, with a horse?'

'There you go again,' replied the Doctor. 'A moment ago you were going on about a little boy.'

They all burst out laughing. Pegoraro remarked:

'Emilito is very fickle.'

Gauna looked up and saw a shooting-star in the sky. He prayed to return to Clara.

Following Valerga's lead they left the path and penetrated into undulating ground – so he thought – on the right. He made his way with difficulty, because the ground, dry and soft, kept yielding beneath his feet.

'What a foul smell,' he exclaimed, 'I can't breathe.'

The whole area seemed redolent of this repulsive smell of sweetish smoke.

'He's so delicate, is Gauna,' remarked Antúnez, putting on a feminine, high-pitched voice.

Gauna heard him from a long way off. A cold sweat moistened his forehead; his vision was blurred. When he came round, he was leaning on the Doctor's arm and the Doctor was saying, in a friendly voice:

'Come on, Emilio. We're nearly there.'

They started walking again. Soon they heard the sound of barking. A pack of stray dogs surrounded them, yapping and whining. As in a dream, he saw a shabbily dressed woman: the woman who had greeted them at the farm in 1927. Now Valerga was arguing with her; he took her by the arm, pushed her aside and made them go in.

The room was small and sordid. Gauna saw a sheepskin in a corner. He let himself fall on top of it and fell asleep.

XLII

When he woke up, the room was dark. He could hear the breathing of people who were asleep. He blocked up his ears, shut his eyes and fell back into the same dream he had been dreaming before he woke up. Armed only with a small knife he was facing a circle of men half hidden in the interlaced pattern of shadows. Gradually by the light of the moon he recognized who they were – the Doctor and the boys. He woke up again and stared into the darkness. Why was he involved in a fight, and why, in his dream, was he so consumed with violent hatred of the Doctor? He no longer heard the slow breathing of those around him. His whole being, tense with the effort, was searching for a memory. He had recaptured it in his dream, and now on waking he had lost it. He must recapture it again. Yes ... that time with the little boy. In the dream he had lived again through that time of the carnival of 1927. Now Gauna could summon it clearly into his memory.

There was not one boy, but two. One of them, three or four years old, dressed as a pierrot, suddenly appeared at their table, weeping silently; another, a little older, was at a table near by. The Doctor was telling a story when the first boy appeared and stopped at his side.

'What's the matter with you, recruit?' asked the Doctor irritably.

The boy went on crying. The Doctor spotted the other child: he called him over, said a few words in his ear and gave him a fifty-centavos note. This other boy, obviously obeying an order, kicked the one dressed as a pierrot and then ran back to the safety of his table. The one in pierrot costume, whose mouth had struck the marble of the table, stood up again, wiped the blood from his lips and went on weeping in silence. Gauna questioned him: the child was lost, and wanted to get back to his parents. The Doctor then rose to his feet, said 'Just a minute, boys', picked the child up in his arms and went out of the café with him. After a moment or two he came back rubbing his hands and said, 'Well, that's that.' He had, he explained, put the boy on the first tram that came along, which happened to be full of people in masks. 'You should have seen how frightened the poor little recruit was,' he added, drawing in his breath.

That was the story of the little boy. That was the first adventure, one fragment, perhaps, of what had become in retrospect the climactic experience of his whole life, those three heroic nights of 1927. And now, what was it that had happened with a horse? 'We were in a victoria,' he said to himself, trying to visualize the scene. He shut his eyes and pressed a hand against his forehead. But it was no good. He could remember nothing. The spell was broken; he was merely an observer of his own mental processes, and they refused to function. Or rather, they refused to obey his will. He found he could visualize not the episode with the horse but only one scene of another episode. A heavily made-up woman was sitting at a wicker table. She wore a light-blue dressing-gown, under which he could see a blouse edged with black lace and embroidered with a heart. She was examining the unknown man's hands, and cried out: 'White spots on the nails ... full of energy today, drained of it tomorrow.' There was music playing. Somebody told him it was *Clair de Lune*. Now it all flooded back vividly to Gauna. He remembered that room, in calle Godoy Cruz. It had an entrance door filled with coloured glass, dark plants in mosaic-covered pots, vast mirrors and lamps covered with red silk shades. He remembered the rose-coloured light and above all, he remembered *Clair de Lune* and the emotion that the music aroused in him. It was being played by a blind

161

violinist, standing framed in the doorway. His head, bent over his instrument, stirred something in Gauna's memory. Where had he seen that sorrowful face before? His hair was brown, long, and wavy: his eyes were sad and wide open; his skin was pale; finally, he had a short, thin beard. At his side a little boy with a hat (undoubtedly the violinist's) pulled down over his ears, was holding a china bowl, collecting money. Seeing the boy Gauna had thought 'Poor Christ, holding a spittoon! It's enough to make you die of laughing.' But he did not laugh. The music of *Clair de Lune* had given him an urge to fraternize with all those present, all mankind, an irrepressible urge towards goodness, a melancholy desire to become a better man. With a lump in his throat and tears rising in his eyes, he told himself that the Sorcerer would have made a new man of him if only he had not died. When the violinist finished, he decided, he would explain to his friends what an extraordinary privilege he had enjoyed in knowing Larsen, and having been able to count on his friendship. But he never actually got as far as this explanation. When *Clair de Lune* came to an end he had forgotten his intention and could only say in a humble voice:

'One more little waltz, maestro.'

But he did not hear the violinist again, at least not that evening. From a nearby room came the sound of a row. He discovered afterwards that an argument over money had broken out between the Doctor, who considered himself wronged, and the owner. The Doctor maintained he had been robbed and the woman kept repeating that they were all honest people: to end the discussion the Doctor, spurred on by the applause of the boys, had gently knocked the woman down, held her by her ankles, and head downwards, shaken her. A few coins did fall out, and the Doctor picked them up. What happened after that was breathtaking. Gauna had just asked the blind man to play again, when the glass door opened noisily and the Doctor and the boys burst in. The Doctor rushed towards the doorway where the blind man was standing; he then noticed the boy, grabbed the bowl from him, emptied out the coins and rammed the bowl down on the blind man's head. There were loud cries. The Doctor shouted: 'Make a dash for it, Emilio,' and they ran along the corridors and then along the street, perhaps pursued by the police. On his way out, Gauna glimpsed the terrified face of the blind man and the veil of blood trickling down his forehead.

XLIII

It was cold in the room. Gauna curled up in the sheep-skin. He opened his eyes to see if he could find something to cover himself with. It was no longer completely dark. Light was coming in through chinks round the door and gaps in the walls. Gauna got up, threw the sheepskin over his shoulders, opened the door and looked out. He thought of Clara and the sunrises they had seen together. Beneath a violet sky, where caves of marble and of glass were lapped by pale emerald lakes, dawn was breaking. A yellowish dog wandered lazily up to him, other dogs were lying asleep. He looked around him: he was standing among hills of brown earth, as though in the centre of a vast, undulating ant-hill. In the distance he could make out a thin column of smoke. There was still a nauseating smell of sweetish smoke.

He walked out and looked back at the house he had slept in: it was a tin shack. There were other shacks not far off. He realized he was in the place where the rubbish was burnt. To the north he could make out the ravines, the pines and the crosses of the cemetery at Flores; further off, the factory he had seen the night before, with its chimneys. Scattered over the rolling surface of the area where the burning was done, he could see a few men sifting through the rubbish. He remembered that during the carnival, after they had spent the night at the farm of the Doctor's friend, they had travelled in a rubbish cart; in his mind's eye he could see the rain falling on the dirty sides of the cart. With a sudden flash of revelation he guessed that the friend's farm was the very same shack in which he had just slept. 'What a state I must have been in,' he thought, 'to have taken it for a farm'. He went on thinking: 'That's why we went in the rubbish-cart; what other vehicles would there be here, apart from the hearses that go to the cemetery? So that's why the Doctor was amazed when I spoke of the farm.'

Then a man on a horse appeared. The hand holding the reins rested on a half-filled bag he carried in front of him, propped up against the animal's neck; in his right hand he had a long stick ending in a nail, which he used to pick up certain selected bits of rubbish and place them in the bag. Looking at that weary horse, with its large pricked-up ears, Gauna remembered another horse, that of the victoria that had taken them from Villa Luro to Flores and then to Nueva Pompeya. Antúnez had sat on the box, singing *Noche de Reyes* and drinking from a bottle of gin he had bought in a shop.

'That poor boy's going to break his neck,' Valerga had remarked, seeing how the drunken Antúnez was rolling around on the box. 'Oh well, let him kill himself.'

To keep himself from falling, Antúnez held on to the driver, who, unable to drive, protested and moaned. The victoria zig-zagged on its way. Valerga softly hummed: '*Poor unhappy mother/Sing a doleful tune.*'

The barber Massantonio wanted to jump off; he was insisting they were going to crash, and was wringing his hands and crying. Gauna ordered the driver to stop, got on to the box and put Antúnez on the seat behind. The Doctor took the bottle from Antúnez's hands, checked that it was empty, and, with excellent aim, sent it flying against a metal post.

From his high seat, Gauna watched the bony horse concentrating on its trot. He looked at its thin, dark hindquarters, its almost horizontal neck, its resigned and narrow forehead and its long, floppy ears covered in sweat.

'The horse seems a good one,' he said, choosing a deliberately understated phrase to express the intense compassion with which he was overwhelmed.

'He doesn't seem, he is,' declared the driver with pride. 'I've known plenty of horses in my life, but never one like Noventa. Of course you're seeing him when he's tired.'

'He's bound to be tired with this long journey,' said Gauna.

'On top of what we'd already done, don't forget. He's pulling us out of pure goodness of heart,' the driver assured him. 'Any other horse would have given up after half the distance. Got a lot of willpower too. But I can tell you he's about to collapse.'

'Have you had him a long time?'

'I bought him at Echepareborda on the 11th of September 1919. And don't you imagine he's had a life of luxury, gorging on fodder. I've always said if he'd just been able to get a sniff of maize from time to time, Noventa wouldn't have needed to be jealous of horses in the best stables in Buenos Aires.'

Now there were no longer houses on either side. They were going down an unmade-up road between vague pastures. Sometimes the moon was hidden behind thick clouds, at others it shone out in the sky. There was that repulsive smell of sweetish smoke.

Something was happening in front. The horse had begun an irregular walk, very calm, something between a walk and a trot. The driver pulled on the reins; the horse immediately stopped.

'What's the matter?' asked the Doctor.

'The horse can't go on like this,' explained the driver. 'Be reasonable, Señor; he's got to have a rest.'

Valerga asked sternly:

'And may I ask by what right you are asking me to be reasonable?'

'My horse is going to drop dead, Señor,' insisted the driver. 'When he starts trotting like that, it's a sign that he's at his last gasp.'

'Your obligation is to take us to our destination. There was a reason for your putting your flag down and the taximeter has been clicking away at ten centavos a time.'

'You can call a policeman if you want. I'm not going to kill my horse for you or for anyone else.'

'And if I kill you, do you think your horse is going to arrange the funeral? You'd better tell your horse to get trotting. All this chat is making me lose my patience.'

The discussion had gone on in the same tone. Finally the driver resigned himself to touching his horse lightly with the whip, and the horse to continuing trotting. But very soon it stumbled and fell, gave an almost human groan and lay stretched on the ground. The carriage stopped with a violent jerk. They all got down and surrounded the horse.

'Oh my God,' exclaimed the driver. 'He's never going to get up again.'

'What do you mean – he's not going to get up?' asked the Doctor, speaking with energy.

The driver did not seem to hear him. He stared fixedly at his horse. Finally he said:

'No, he's not going to get up. He's had it. Oh my poor Noventa!'

'I'm off,' announced Massantonio. He could not keep still and seemed on the verge of a nervous attack.

'That's enough,' Valerga ordered him.

Almost in tears, the barber insisted:

'But I've got to go, Señor. What on earth is my wife going to say when she sees me coming back tomorrow morning? I'm off.'

Valerga said to him:

'You're staying here.'

'You've had it, my poor old horse, you've had it,' the driver was repeating, inconsolable. He seemed incapable of taking a decision or of doing anything for his horse. He gazed at it pathetically, shaking his head.

'If this man says it's had it, I reckon we should consider it as dead,' declared Antúnez gravely.

'And what shall we do after that?' asked Pegoraro. 'Is the driver going to take us piggy-back?'

'That's another question altogether,' Antúnez retorted. 'One thing at a time. Right now I'm talking about the horse called Noventa. I think it should be finished off with a bullet.'

Antúnez had a revolver in his hand. He looked at the

eyes of the horse stretched out on the ground. By the pain and the sadness expressed in those eyes, the animal showed that it was still clinging avidly to life. It was horrible that there they were talking of killing it.

'I'll give you two pesos for the carcass,' Antúnez said to the driver, who was listening to him in a daze. 'I'll buy it from you for my old man, the poor thing's a bit of a dreamer. He had visions of setting up a company some day to take dead animals to bits and sell the bits separately: skin in one place, fat in another, if you see what I mean. With the bones and the blood, me and my old man would make a first-class fertilizer. You won't believe me, but as regards fertilizers ...'

Valerga interrupted him:

'Why are you talking about sacrificing a horse that is in a perfectly good state of conservation? All we have to do is get him on his legs again.'

'If we don't ,' pointed out Pegoraro, 'who will transport us, calm and comfortably seated, to our destination?'

'It's all useless,' the driver repeated. 'My Noventa is dying.'

Gauna said: 'We should release it from the shafts.'

With great difficulty, they succeeded in releasing it. Then they pushed the carriage backwards. The doctor picked up the reins, and ordered Gauna to take the whip. 'Now!' shouted the Doctor, and he tugged; Gauna, with the whip, tried to rouse the horse. The Doctor began getting impatient. Each tug on the reins was more brutal than the previous one.

'What's the matter with you?' the Doctor asked Gauna, with an indignant look. 'Don't you know how to use a whip or are you feeling sorry for the horse?'

All that pulling had damaged the animal's mouth. Injured by the bit, the corners of its mouth were bleeding. Depths of immovable calm seemed reflected in the sadness of its eyes. Whatever happened, he would not use the whip against the horse again. 'If necessary,' he thought, 'I'll use it against the Doctor.' The driver began weeping.

'I shall never find a horse like this one,' he groaned, 'not even for sixty pesos.'

168

'Come on now,' Valerga said to him, 'What's the use of crying? I'm doing all I can but I must warn you not to try my patience.'

'I'm off,' said Massantonio.

Valerga turned to the boys:

'I'll pull on the reins and you, all together, lift it off the ground.'

Gauna put the whip on the ground and got ready to help.

'That's no longer a mouth,' remarked Valerga, 'it's just a mass of flesh. If I pull, I'll demolish it.'

Valerga pulled hard, the others pushed and, between them, they got the horse on its feet. They surrounded it, shouting: 'Hurrah!' 'Long live Noventa!' 'Long live Platense!', slapping each other on the back and leaping around in joy.

Valerga spoke to the driver.

'You see, my friend. There was no need to start crying so soon.'

'I'm going to put it back in the shafts,' announced Pegoraro.

Maidana intervened:

'Don't be a brute,' he said. 'That poor horse is half-dead. At least let him get his breath back.'

'Sod that,' protested Antúnez, brandishing the revolver. 'We're not going to spend the night in the open.'

Pegoraro good-humouredly suggested:

'Maybe he'd like us to harness him instead.'

He pushed the carriage towards the horse. With his free hand, Antúnez tried to help him; he took the reins and gave a pull. The horse fell down again.

Valerga picked up the whip that was on the ground and brandished it at Antúnez.

'I should use this on you,' he told him. 'You're scum. The scum of the earth.'

He grabbed the reins from him, turned to the driver and spoke to him calmly:

'Frankly, Governor, it seems to me that your horse is trying to make fools of us. I'm going to cure him of his bad habits.'

With his left hand he tugged upwards and with the right he brought the whip brutally down on the animal, one lash after another. The horse gave a terrible groan; its whole body shuddered as it tried to get up; it nearly made it, was overcome by trembling, and collapsed again.

'For pity's sake, Señor, for pity's sake,' exclaimed the driver.

The horse's eyes seemed to start out of their sockets in a frenzy of fear. Valerga raised the whip again but, before it descended, Gauna went up to Antúnez, wrenched the revolver from him, held the barrel against the horse's forehead, and with eyes wide open, fired.

XLIV

Gauna, leaning against the door of the shack, gazing at the dawn which was breaking over the city beyond the smouldering rubbish-dump, wondered whether those were the forgotten and magical episodes of 1927, that now, after three years of intermittent, secretive and fervent searching, he had managed to recapture. As in the mirrors of a labyrinth, he had found in this carnival of 1930, three events of the other carnival. Was it necessary to go right to the end? Did he have to penetrate to the very source of its murky brilliance before he could solve the mystery and lay bare its hateful sordidness?

How humiliating, he thought. How humiliating to have spent these three years longing to relive those moments, just as one longs to relive some wonderful dream – only in this case it was not a dream but the culmination of his whole life – and then, when he was finally able to dredge some part of that glorious past out of the depths, what did he actually see? The incident of the horse. Episodes of the most squalid cruelty. How could mere oblivion have converted them into something precious, something he longed to recapture?

Why had he ever got on well with the gang? Why had he admired Valerga? To think that he had actually ditched Clara to go out with these people ... He shut his eyes and clenched his fists. He had to get his own back for the vile deeds they had led him into. He had to tell Valerga how much he despised him.

He gazed into the infinite blue of the sky. The fantastic

architecture of the dawn, made up of clouds and clear depths, had now disappeared. The morning was beginning. Gauna ran a hand over his forehead. It was moist and cold. He felt immensely tired. He realized, in a rapid and confused fashion, that he should not seek revenge or look for a fight. He just wanted to be a long way away. He wanted to forget these people, as one wants to forget a nightmare. He would go back to Clara. At once.

Of course, he did not go back. Once again he goaded himself to the old facile anger, repeating to himself, 'Those bastards are going to find out what I think of them,' but very soon his energy subsided, and he was overcome by a feeling of apathy. It gave him a sort of subtle, indefinable happiness to surrender himself once more to his fate. He knew, I believe, that if he gave up his quest half-finished he would regret it for the rest of his life. He leaned against the door of the shack, conscious of time passing, and imagining himself as a cunning card-player who calmly and unhurriedly ponders his cards and, because he does not get impatient, is unbeatable. Again, he tried to turn his mind back to the 1927 carnival, but he was distracted by his present feelings and by his flattering image of himself as a card-player. Nevertheless, since our thoughts follow mysterious paths and can take unexpected short cuts, in the middle of all this vagueness, Gauna suddenly found that he knew who the blind violinist was – the man whom he had so inexplicably (as it had seemed to him then) terrified, in the courtyard of the house in Barracas the day Clara had told him about going out with Baumgarten: he was the same man the Doctor had attacked in calle Godoy Cruz. The blind man had been frightened because he recognized his voice: before Valerga had attacked him, he, Gauna, had asked him, as afterwards at Barracas, to play another little waltz. As for the bitterness he felt now, there was no mystery about that; it arose from the memory of what for Gauna had been Clara's completely baffling volte-face.

The yellowish dog came up to him again. Gauna took a step forward to stroke him, and the step echoed painfully in his head, like a stone thrown in the still water of a lake.

After a while the boys and the Doctor emerged from the shack, squinting with half-closed eyes and with pained expressions, as though the dazzle of the day was blinding them. The morning passed lazily by. Someone got hold of a bottle of gin; lying in the shade of the cart, they shared it. Gauna was bothered by the acrid, sickly smell of the burning rubbish. The others were not, and they teased Gauna about his over-sensitivity. As they dozed, green flies buzzed around their tired, aching heads.

Towards the end of the afternoon, the owner of the place arrived on horseback, accompanied by four or five workmen on foot, in shirtsleeves and wearing baggy trousers. The boss wore a city suit, with cycle-clips around the bottoms of his trousers. He was a robust man of about fifty, with a big, cheerful, clean-shaven face, and a frank open smile which nevertheless contained a hint now and again that he was not entirely to be trusted. His hair was close-cropped at the back and sides; his short arms, stomach and legs were fat. On greeting the Doctor he bent forward from the waist and let his arms hang down, like a puppet with a hinge in the middle. His business was sifting rubbish, concentrating in particular on medical products. He had become a kind of entrepreneur, employing a team of workers who spread out over the area where the burning was taking place and prospected for him. He greeted Valerga with a cordiality that was a shade pompous; the boys he virtually ignored.

'How's it going, Don Ponciano?' asked the Doctor.

'Well, as you realize, my friend, it's a profession like any other. Chance may bring you a period of affluence, only to be succeeded by another, much longer period, with all due respect, of sheer misery. But I don't complain. The real thorn in my side, if you follow me, the fly in the ointment, is my work-force. I pay them like kings, according to the wage-structure that is customary in the salvage industry, you understand, and the pay fluctuates with the amount collected. But they give me headaches such that no painkiller ever produced in Argentina can relieve. Believe me when I tell you that I am simply stagnating here; and lament my fate. I, who honour all that is right, beautiful and true – they make a shambles of my life by appropriating things that do not belong to them, invading the territory of a colleague, who then comes down on *me* with a great rusty knife as if it were *I* who had committed the offence. Imagine a gentleman who lives by prospecting for gold, and who has found nothing but a handful of dust. What sort of view is he going to take of these fellows of mine, grinning like princes, with their mouths full of gold teeth?'

The Doctor must have been very fond of his friend, since he let him go on talking, without any protest, to the point of exhaustion. The boys were lost in admiration at this proof of tolerance, and they swore, frequently crossing themselves, that they had never seen the Doctor so peaceable and good-humoured as during this carnival. There followed a brief dispute between the Doctor and his friend, in the course of which the former never betrayed the least irritation: the friend was inviting everyone to partake of his meal and the Doctor, out of politeness, would not hear of it. The woman who had received them so ungraciously the evening before, soon arrived with some meat. While it was being grilled – Gauna's eyes were fixed on the little lead balls oozing out of the pot on the fire – the boss was collecting the bags handed to him by his employees, and paying them. The meal – leathery steaks, ship's biscuits and beer – went on until very late. The important thing was the mood of relaxed cordiality. The boss invited them to a fancy-dress ball that evening in a house in avenida Cruz.

'The guests,' he explained, 'will be from the top drawer. The host, who's a tycoon, knows how to live. He understands life, if you see what I mean, and he recruits the women from Villa Soldati and Villa Crespo. I've got a free hand: I can invite anyone I like because he thinks the world of me. He's an interesting man to meet. Entirely self-made, pulled himself up by his own boot-straps, collecting cotton waste, an extremely profitable commodity, which otherwise just gets thrown away. Need I add that the man to whom I refer is a foreigner, one of those thrifty types who know the value of every penny?'

The Doctor said that unfortunately neither he nor the boys could come to the ball because they had to be on their way to Barrracas that evening. The friend offered to put in a word with the driver of the dust-cart. He explained:

'We don't usually get on very well together, we of the private sector and those parasites who live off our taxes and who wear official badges on their caps. But I get on well with everybody, and if you go to the ball tonight, tomorrow, when the man starts his round, he'll give you a lift in his cart, and you can travel more comfortably. I'm 95 per cent certain I can get you transport for tomorrow.'

Not even this assurance could induce Valerga and Gauna to stay; but it all worked out well. The driver of the cart turned up a moment later, leading two piebald horses on reins arranged like a halter.

'I've got to harness them,' he said to Don Ponciano.

The dust-carts were going to give the city, littered with streamers from the afternoon's festivities, a bit of a clean. Don Ponciano asked him:

'Could you give these friends of mine a lift?'

'I'm heading for avenida Montes de Oca,' the driver replied. 'If that suits you, fine.'

'Yes, it does suit us,' replied the Doctor.

XLV

When the man had harnessed the cart, the Doctor and the boys said goodbye to Don Ponciano. Then they got in – the Doctor and the carter on the driver's box, Gauna and the boys in the back.

They went along avenida Cruz, and then turned right down avenida La Plata, where the parades were beginning to get lively again; in calle Almafuerte, Gauna saw a shrine with an image of Santa Rita; it struck him that it was easier to imagine death than to imagine the time when the world would go on without him. They went down Famatina and avenida Alcorta which brought them to a gloomy neighbourhood of factories and gasometers; in avenida Sáenz, some groups of masqueraders, small groups, and noisy, reminded them that it was carnival time; they went along Perdriel, and going down the hill in calle Bransden they went past walls, railings and melancholy gardens, full of eucalyptus and casuarinas.

'The Hospice of Las Mercedes,' explained Pegoraro.

Gauna wondered how he could have believed that with these three days of carnival he would recapture what he had felt the previous time, that he would be once again in the carnival of 1927. There can only be one present: that is what he had not realized, and that is why his feeble attempts at invocatory magic had failed.

They stopped in calle Vieytes, beside the statue. The Doctor got down and said to them:

'We'll stop here.'

While the driver tied the reins to the bar around the

176

coachman's seat and put the brake on, Valerga, pointing to the restaurant and grill-room, El Antiguo Sola, explained to the boys:

'You eat well here. The food is simple, but well prepared. A taxi-driver recommended it to me around 1923 – they get around, those drivers, and they know about good eating. Later I learned that a brother of the proprietor works in an olive-oil business. So they're not mean with the good stuff. And do you know what that's worth these days? It's more than money can buy. And on top of that, as the neighbourhood is rather out of the way, we may be free of masqueraders, bands and other such things. There's a place for everything, isn't there? Digestion needs calm.'

Valerga invited the driver in for a drink. They drank their rums up at the bar while the boys waited for them at a table. The proprietor did not seem to recognize Valerga but this did not offend him and, when the driver had gone, he began recommending the oil, the meat and the mortadella in the manner of a regular client and a connoisseur.

To start with they had mortadella, salami and raw ham, followed by a selection of cold meats with a mixed salad. Valerga said:

'Don't forget to check whether they've emptied the oil out of the sewing-machine.'

Red wine followed. After that the waiter offered them cheese and dulce.

'Dulce's a policeman's dessert – bring us cheese,' replied Valerga.

A band of four musicians, dressed as devils, came in. Before they could begin clashing their cymbals, Gauna handed them a peso, explaining by way of excuse:

'I'd rather waste a peso than have us deafened by that racket.'

'If it's the expense you're worried about, we can pass the hat,' remarked Maidana sarcastically.

While the devils thanked them and made their farewells, Valerga declared:

'It seems to me unwise to invest in imbeciles.'

They ended the meal with fruit and coffee. Before leaving, Gauna went to the gents. Scrawled in pencil on a wall was the phrase: 'For the proprietor'. Gauna wondered whether Valerga had been there; but he had drunk so much red wine that he could remember nothing.

They walked a bit to get some fresh air. The Doctor turned to Antúnez:

'Come on then, haven't you got any feeling? On a night like this, I'd start singing at the top of my lungs, if I could. Go on, sing us *Don Juan*.'

While Antúnez launched into *Don Juan*, as well as he could, Valerga, looking at some little old one-storey houses, remarked:

'When are they going to put up factories and mills here instead of these hovels?'

Maidana was bold enough to suggest an alternative:

'Or nice little houses for workers.'

XLVI

They began feeling thirsty and, making jokes about their dryness, comparing their throats to an engine that has seized up, or to sandpaper, they reached El Aeroplano bar opposite plaza Díaz Vélez. Near their table there were two men drinking: one leaning against the bar and the other with his elbows on a table. The one at the bar was tall, cheerful and relaxed looking, with his hat tilted back. The other was not so thin and was blond, with very fair skin, thoughtful, sad, light blue eyes and a blond moustache.

'Listen, friend,' the fair-haired one was explaining in a loud voice, as though he wanted everyone to hear him, 'the fate of this country is pretty strange. Tell me, what is Argentina known for the world over?'

'Brilliantine,' replied the one at the bar. 'Tragacanth gum, that comes from India.'

'Come on now, don't be a fool. I'm being serious. Let's weigh it all up: I'm not talking about wealth, since before the economic recovery and the sanitation programme, we were already a complete wash-out compared with the Yankees; nor about physical size, since not even the most partisan can deny that Brazil is twice as big; nor about the quantity of cattle or agricultural produce, because if you think about it there's more in the smallest market in Chicago than in the great granary of our Republic; nor about maté, that drink which comes in sacks from Brazil and Paraguay; and I've no wish to bore the pants off you with tales of books, not even with the greatest glory of our

179

scribblers, the *criolladas** – Martín Fierro brand – which were invented by none other than Hidalgo, a fellow from across the river.'‡

The young man at the bar replied with a yawn:

'OK. You've told me what you're not going to talk about, now tell me what you are. I sometimes wonder, Amaro, whether you aren't becoming a real old Spanish windbag.'

'Don't ever say that to me, not even as a joke. It's precisely because I'm every bit as true a native of Buenos Aires as you, even though I don't wear my hat tilted back, that I'm confiding these truths to you, with a heart that is burning my fingers like the fried potatoes that are sold in Paseo de Julio. It's enough to make you despair, Arocena. What I'm talking about are not trivialities. I'm talking about things that are real, legitimate reasons for our pride, which spring from the heart of our people: I'm talking about the tango and about football. Listen – and this is between you and me: according to the late lamented Rossi, defender of all that is ours, who lived in Córdoba but was in fact a Uruguayan, the tango, our own tango, more Argentine than a bad smell, our ambassador to the world, danced in Europe and praised by the Pope himself, originated in Montevideo.'

'I admit that once you start listening to Uruguayans, all of us Argentines were born there, from Florencio Sánchez to Horacio Quiroga.'

'Well, there must be a reason for it. Not to mention Gardel, whom, if he's not French, I consider Uruguayan, nor the fact that the most famous tango of all is claimed by them too.'

'I can't take any more of this,' Gauna burst out. 'Forgive my butting in but no matter how unpatriotic you are, you can't compare that rubbish with *Ivette*, *Una noche de garufa*, *La Catrera*, *El porteñito* and many more.'

---

*Typical Argentines
‡i.e. from Uruguay

'There's no need to get excited, young man, or to act as if you were a publicity agent for our tango publishers: I didn't say it was the best, I said it was the most famous.' Then as though forgetting about Gauna, he went on talking to the man at the bar. 'And as far as football is concerned, the sport we play right from the cradle, in the street and with a bag of beans; the sport we're all crazy about, government and opposition alike, and that has made us travel round in lorries yelling to uninvolved passers-by 'Bo-ca! Bo-ca!' – as far as this sport, that's made us famous the whole world over is concerned, we've got to face it: time and again the Uruguayans wipe the floor with us, *they* are the Olympic champions and *they* are the world champions.'

'And what about horse-racing?' demanded the man at the bar. 'I'm not saying I agree with you, but I reckon Torlerolo or Leguisamo are Uruguayan, or very nearly so.'

And having said that, the one called Arocena grabbed a ham-and-cheese sandwich from under a glass bell, and added:

'Perhaps my memory will come back to me with the help of this reinforcement.'

The Doctor remarked in a low voice:

'I'm sure something is going on here.' He paused and then went on: 'At this moment I don't find it at all easy to control myself, but I don't believe in verbal rebukes.'

Forgetting his resentment, Gauna looked at him with all his original admiration intact, wanting to believe in the hero and his mythology, and hoping that real life, aware of his innermost, fervent desires, would at last present him with the episode he wanted. That episode was not exactly essential to his faith, but it would bear witness to it, as miracles do to believers in other faiths. Resplendently it would confirm him in his first calling, and enable him, after so many contradictions, to go on believing in the romantic and blessed hierarchy that places courage above every other virtue.

Meanwhile the boy with the hat round his neck was saying something; he was saying:

'And after all, we've not only got a reputation in these

god-forsaken lands: night-clubs in France and California are full of Argentines with slicked-down hair who live by introducing you to women who, frankly, you'd have to be blind to take up.'

'And what's that got to do with the guys from the other side?' asked the one who was leaning on the table.

'What do you mean, what's it got to do with them? They're all called Julio and they're all Uruguayans.'

'Now we shall be told that we Argentines aren't even any good with women,' said the Doctor. Raising his voice, he ordered: 'Waiter, bring these gentlemen a drink, and let them tell us why we're such a hopeless case. They must know.'

The two men asked for brandy with cherries.

'Uruguayan, please: what you get here isn't much good,' the blond man told the waiter.

'A very light drink,' commented Pegoraro.

'A woman's drink,' added Antúnez.

'This gentleman here is known as El Largo or El Pasaje Barolo,' said Maidana rapidly, pointing to Antúnez. 'He's over six feet tall. Do you think that if you combed Montevideo with a magnifying glass you'd find a monument like El Pasaje Barolo? I wouldn't know, as I've never been there, and have no intention of going.'

The Doctor explained to Gauna in a low voice:

'The boys are like hounds, hunting hounds, that lead you to the quarry, or more often make you lose it. You'll see, any minute now they'll start throwing crumbs or lumps of sugar at them.'

That did not happen; there was no time. All at once, the man with the hat around his neck said:

'Good night, gentlemen. Many thanks.'

The blond one also said: 'Many thanks,' and they both made a peaceful exit. The Doctor got up to follow them.

'Leave them alone, Doctor,' Gauna interceded. 'Let them go. A moment ago I was hoping you'd go for them; but now I'm not.'

The Doctor let him finish; then he took a step towards the door. Gauna held his arm in a gesture of persuasion.

The Doctor looked with hatred at the hand that was touching him.

'Please,' said Gauna. 'If you go after them, Doctor, you'll kill them. The carnival goes on until tomorrow. Don't let's interrupt our celebrations for the sake of those total strangers. I am asking you, and don't forget that you are my guest.'

'And after all,' ventured Antúnez, wanting to smooth over an awkward situation, 'it all happened among Argentines. If they'd been foreigners, then we couldn't have forgiven the insult.'

'Who the hell asked your opinion?' the Doctor shouted at him furiously.

With a feeling of gratitude, Gauna reflected that Valerga always treated him with respect.

XLVII

They went down Osvaldo Cruz until they reached Montes de Oca. The establishment they had visited in 1927 was now a family house. Maidana said:

'I wonder what the girls here now are like.'

'Just like all the others,' replied Antúnez.

'With a certain *difference*,' added Pegoraro.

'I can't see anything special,' said Antúnez.

'The boys round here must make all sorts of allusions, to amuse them,' Maidana went on.

They went into several cafés. The Doctor seemed offended with Gauna. Gauna looked at him with renewed affection which had something filial in it. He was almost upset by Valerga's resentment, but it did not bother him too much. The vital thing was their reconciliation, the spirit of friendship he now felt. It was not the exhaustion resulting from his chaotic day, nor the many drinks, that made him forget the bad feelings of the morning; it was undoubtedly the feelings aroused in the bar in plaza Díaz Vélez, when the conversation of those strangers had disturbed and, as it were, humiliated many of his most cherished beliefs, and when Valerga, true to himself or to the idea Gauna had had of him at the very beginning, had risen up like a tower of courage.

Around Montes de Oca they looked for a hotel to spend the night. They almost went into the one at Guimares and Moreyra but when they saw there was a garage underneath it, they went on.

'We'd do better to go and look up Araujo the cripple,' said Valerga.

The cripple Araujo was the owner, or rather the caretaker, of a builder's merchants in calle Lamadrid. The boys were amazed. Shaking their heads, they commented on the incredible fact. Pegoraro pointed out to them:

'A man from Saavedra, like the Doctor, with a network of acquaintances in the remotest places, and even in neighbourhoods far from the centre, not to say peripheral!'

'And yet as much a part of Saavedra as the park itself,' added Antúnez.

'Doesn't seem extraordinary to me,' ventured Maidana. 'We're from Saavedra, yet here we are.'

'Don't be a fool,' remonstrated Pegoraro, 'things are different today.'

'That boy,' said Antúnez, pointing to Maidana, 'with his mania for finding fault, has no respect for anyone.'

Pegoraro caught up with the Doctor, who was walking in front with Gauna, and asked him:

'How do you manage to have so many acquaintances, Doctor?'

'When you've all lived as long as I have, my boy,' replied Valerga, with a kind of melancholy pride, 'you'll see that though you may not have played the big parts you'll have collected a crowd of friends, if that's what you like to call them, who in your hour of need will not refuse you shelter for the night, even if it's only in this rat-infested yard.'

While the Doctor was knocking at the door, Gauna thought: 'If it were anyone else, Providence would get its own back for that boast by seeing to it that he doesn't get in; but the Doctor's the kind of person that never happens to.' And indeed it did not happen. Araujo approached, interminably slowly as it seemed, limping and grumbling. He eventually opened the door, and was in the middle of greeting the Doctor when he noticed the boys in the shadows and drew back, almost imperceptibly, in alarm. The Doctor leant against the door, perhaps to prevent his friend from shutting it, and spoke to him calmly:

'Don't be frightened, Don Araujo. We haven't come to attack you today. These gentlemen here have come to honour the carnival with their presence, and what do you think, they had the kindness to ask this old man to join them. Well, night has descended on us and I thought: before going to a hotel, I ought to remember my old friend Araujo.'

'And quite right you were to do so,' declared Araujo, who was now reassured. 'Perfectly right.'

The Doctor went on:

'At our age, we're over the hill. If you go out with young people, the best you can hope for is to be taken for a schoolmaster taking his pupils for a walk. If, on the other hand, you go out with people of your own age, you find yourself sitting in the sun on a bench in the square bawling into someone's ear. I think there's nothing left for us but to sit down alone and drink our maté until the undertaker comes.'

Limping and coughing, Araujo protested that destiny had livelier entertainments and many years of life in store for the two of them.

They discussed how they would install themselves for the night.

'I can't offer you anything luxurious,' the cripple went on. 'For the Doctor, there's the little sofa in the study. I'm afraid you really won't find it very comfortable, but there's nothing better in the house. I've tried it out myself in the past: I'd stretch out there occasionally for a little nap and you should have seen me the next day: I'd get up more bent than an old hunchback. I suspect that rheumatism isn't the result of badly positioned furniture, as some people claim, but of squashing one's head up against the back of the sofa. I'll get some clean sacks for the gentlemen. Find a corner and stretch out – make yourselves at home.'

Gauna was very tired. He had a confused memory of having groped his way in the darkness among white shapes. He must have fallen asleep very soon after.

He dreamed he entered a candle-lit hall in which there was a huge round table at which the heroes were sitting,

186

playing cards. He could not see Falucho, or Sergeant Cabral, or anyone he could identify. There were some young boys, half-naked but not savage, and their faces and bodies were so white that they seemed to be made of plaster. They reminded him of the statue of the Discus Thrower in the Platense Club. The cards they were using were twice as big as normal and – another notable fact – they were those cards that have clubs and hearts. The players were arguing about the right to ascend the throne, that is to say to occupy the place of honour and be considered the greatest among the heroes. The throne was like a chair in a shoe-shine parlour but even higher and more comfortable. Gauna noticed that a long red carpet, like the one there was said to be in the Royal, led right up to the seat. Just as he was trying to understand the meaning of it all he woke up. He found himself lying among statues which, as the lame man explained to him while they were drinking maté, represented Jason and the heroes who had accompanied him on his adventures. Gauna tried to call the attention of the boys to the fact that he had dreamed of those heroes before ever hearing of them or seeing their statues.

'Hasn't anyone told you you're a terrible bore when you talk about your dreams?' Pegoraro asked him.

'I don't know,' replied Gauna.

'Well, it's high time you did,' declared Pegoraro.

Araujo asked if they wouldn't mind leaving a little before eight, as that was when the workmen and the ugly secretary started arriving.

Apologizing, he added: 'Someone will always talk, and the boss might not like it.'

'For all his ceremoniousness,' said the Doctor, 'this bilious old cripple is in fact throwing us out.'

The Doctor was not serious: he merely wanted to humiliate his friend. Araujo protested: 'Don't say that, Doctor! As far as I'm concerned, you're welcome to stay.'

In a café in Montes de Oca around the 600s they breakfasted on coffee, cakes and croissants. Then, near Constitución, they went into a bathhouse, and while 'the Turks made them into new men', as the Doctor put it,

187

their clothes were ironed and brushed. They lunched in luxury in the liveliest part of avenida de Mayo. Then they went to a cinema and saw *The Price of Glory* with Barry Norton, and in the Bataclán a variety show which 'frankly', said Pegoraro, 'was not up to standard'. They dined in a dive in Paseo de Julio. For a few coins they contemplated scenes of the promenade at Mar del Plata, of the Paris exhibition of 1889, of obese Japanese wrestlers in different poses, and others of people of both sexes. Afterwards, in an open Buick taxi they drove along past the parades and arrived at the Armenonville. Before getting out, Pegoraro slashed the red leather upholstery with his penknife. 'I've left my signature,' he said.

There was an awkward moment when the doorman at the Armenonville tried to stop them going in, but Gauna handed him a five-peso note and the doors of that enchanted palace opened to our heroes.

XLVIII

I must now proceed slowly and very carefully. What I have to tell is so strange that if I do not explain it all clearly no one will understand or believe me. Now begins the magical part of this story, or perhaps it has all been magical, only we have failed to perceive its true nature. We may have been misled by the atmosphere of Buenos Aires, sceptical and vulgar.

When Gauna entered the brilliantly lit hall of the Armenonville, when he edged his way along past the colourful, slow-moving sea of masked couples dancing a vague sort of foxtrot modelled on some equally vague foxtrot of bygone years, when he forgot his plan, he believed the longed-for miracle was happening. He believed that not only he but also his friends were in the same state of mind as in 1927. Some people will say that there is nothing very strange in all this: that he had prepared himself psychologically by trying to remember the experience and then forgetting it, as you might leave a door open; that he had prepared himself physically too, for the exhaustion, after three days of walking, drinking and going without sleep must have been the same both times; finally, that the Armenonville, so luxurious, so dazzling, with its lights, its music and its masked girls, was a unique place in his experience. Admittedly this account does seem to describe a psychological fact rather than a magical fact – something that occurred only in Gauna's mind and whose origins should be sought in exhaustion and alcohol. But I suspect that certain events of the last

189

night are still not explained; and I wonder whether those events are not inexplicable or at least magical.

They soon found a table. Each examined the paper hat lying on his napkin. Amid the hilarity and the indifference of the Doctor, Pegoraro tried his on. The others put theirs aside, intending to take them home as souvenirs. They drank a toast in champagne, and as Gauna raised his glass, who should he see drinking at the bar? As he said to himself, he couldn't believe his eyes: it was one of the boys from the Lincoln, the fair-haired one with the big head who had stood in the same place in 1927. Gauna was quite certain that if he looked a little longer he would see the other three: the bow-legged one who had squared up to him like a boxer, the tall pale one, and the one who looked as though he had come out of a book by Grosso. Twice more he filled his glass and gulped it down. But need we remind ourselves who was with those boys at the Armenonville that night in 1927? Of course not. There before Gauna's amazed and incredulous eyes, leaning against the same bar, a little to the right, with a domino identical to the one she was wearing in 1927, there, beyond any shadow of doubt, stood the masked girl.

XLIX

Although he had expected it, the apparition disturbed him so much that he wondered whether it was not an illusion produced by the alcohol. He did not seriously think that – the presence and reality of the girl were tangible – but whatever the reason he was deeply moved, and those last two glasses of champagne had affected him more than all the grappa and rum he had already drunk. That was why he did not try to get up. He waved several times to attract the attention of the masked girl. He hoped she would recognize him and come and sit next to him.

Looking back and forth from the masked girl to Gauna, Pegoraro said: 'She hasn't seen him.'

'I wonder how she can not see him,' said Maidana.

'I really don't know,' proclaimed Pegoraro, 'Gauna is waving so hard he's making me dizzy.'

Maidana declared solemnly: 'I reckon the girl at the bar has mistaken him for the Invisible Man.'

Lost in his thoughts, Gauna wondered: 'What if it isn't her?' In his drunken meanderings he was struck by an almost philosophical doubt. First he thought that the domino and mask might prove a disappointment. Then, with anguish, he glimpsed an alternative possibility that seemed to him original, though perhaps it was not: if you took away the domino and mask, there would be nothing left of the masked girl of 1927, since those features were the most concrete part of his memory. Of course the enchantment remained, but how could one pin down so vague and magical an essence in the memory? He did not know whether this thought should comfort him or make him despair.

The short fair-haired boy went up to the girl; he gazed and smiled at her in wonder. She smiled too, but her expression was more ambiguous, probably because of the mask. Or did that ambiguity only exist in Gauna's imagination? Now the fair-haired boy took her off to dance. The hall was vast. It took a lot of concentration to follow them among the dancing couples but despite the depression that had come over him, Gauna was determined not to lose sight of her. He remembered an evening in Lobos when as a child he had watched the path of the moon among the clouds: a mill was being built and he had climbed the unfinished tower and amused himself predicting the moment when the moon would reappear between large clouds. He got it right of course, and was delighted, and felt a pleasant sense of confidence in the prophetic powers he thought he was discovering in himself.

Suddenly he felt bewildered. Behind the slow swaying of donkey heads and falcon heads that looked like tall helmets, the masked girl had disappeared. Gauna wanted to get up, but was held back by the fear of falling and making himself ridiculous in front of all those strangers. He drank some more to give himself courage.

'I'm going to another table,' he said. 'I've got to talk to a girl I know.'

They made a lot of jokes to which he didn't listen – that he had better be there when the bill came or that he should leave them his wallet – and they roared with laughter as if his standing up was a comic performance. For a moment he forgot the masked girl. Finding a table seemed a difficult and agonizing task. He could not go back to the boys now, and he had nowhere to sit. Feeling very unhappy, he walked as best he could till suddenly, hardly able to believe it, he found himself in front of an empty table. He immediately sank into a chair. Were the boys looking at him? No: he couldn't see them from there so they couldn't see him either. A waiter asked him something. Though he did not hear the words he guessed them and, feeling very happy, he replied: 'Champagne.'

But his troubles were not over. He had not wanted that table in order to be alone – what a disgrace if they see me here alone, he murmured – but other people would take it as soon as he left it; and yet, if he did not find the masked girl, he might lose her for ever.

L

At least one other person in the Armenonville that night shared Gauna's impression that a miracle was happening. However, the two witnesses did not see it in the same way. Gauna had set off in search of the miracle, and when he had almost given up he had found it. The masked girl did not see in this the simple repetition of a state of mind, however miraculous; to her it was an appalling portent. Something more personal, however, concealed that terror from her and made her see what happened as another miracle, infinitely vivid and happy. On this last night of the great adventure Gauna and the girl are like two actors who, as they play their parts, pass beyond the magical situation in a drama into a magical world.

When at last she found Gauna at his distant table, his head in his hands, looking so forlorn and so serious, the masked girl ran towards him. The fair-haired boy, El Rubio, was left alone in the midst of a jostling throng of dancers, wondering whether he should wait there because she had said, 'I'm coming straight back.' The presence of the masked girl rescued Gauna from the depression he had been plunged into by the last few drinks and the crazy adventures of those three days and nights. As for her, she threw caution to the winds, forgot her vow not to drink, and gave herself up to the joy of being once again bewitching to her husband. With these words it is revealed that the masked girl was Clara – the masked girl that night and the one who had dazzled him in 1927.

The evening before – I am of course now speaking of

194

1930 – Don Serafín had appeared to Clara in a dream and had said: 'The third night is going to repeat itself. Protect Emilio.' For Clara this announcement was the definitive, supernatural confirmation of all her fears; but it was not the origin. Everyone in the neighbourhood knew that Gauna had won a lot of money on the races and had gone off with the Doctor and the boys, so how could she not know it too? They knew that in the neighbourhood and they knew something more: the gossips said that Gauna was the chief heir of the Sorcerer, subscribed to the bulletin of the Spiritualist Centre, and that his sinister aim on this expedition was to recover the mad, fantastic visions he had seen, or thought he had seen, on the third night of the carnival of 1927.

And so those days were full of anguish for Clara. Then her courage returned. She would go to the Armenonville to meet Gauna and she would fight for him. She felt full of confidence. Clara was a brave girl, and the prospect of a fight always inspires courage in the brave. She almost stopped worrying, but she had one problem – perhaps only a problem of conscience, one of those problems that are solved by the very act of formulating them and are really just a matter of abandoning scruples and precautions: Clara's problem was to find someone to go with her. She would have liked to go alone, but she knew that when she arrived at the Armenonville alone she might well not be let in. Larsen was of course the obvious choice. He was the only one Gauna would have accepted, the only friend who could be relied upon. She would have to try to convince him, which would not be easy. She would use all her powers of persuasion.

After pondering for a whole night she decided her chances would be better if she spoke spontaneously, at the last minute. She must not get carried away by impatience. Larsen was almost over a cold, and Clara knew all about Larsen and his colds: he would be well by Monday night, she thought, but if she gave him time he would use the cold as an excuse to refuse straightaway or, if he'd agreed, he'd then have a timely relapse.

Eloquence and strategy – what use are they? Larsen

shook his head and solemnly explained about the risk that the catarrh, at present confined to an area below the throat, would, at the slightest provocation, turn into flu. Disappointed, Clara smiled. It is comforting to think of characters like Larsen. They are unshakeable in the midst of change and universal corruption. True to themselves, faithful to their little egoisms, when you look for them you find them.

She did not give up. She could not explain everything to him, however. From the calm of that peaceful late afternoon in their neighbourhood, two old friends having a sensible talk, the explanation would have seemed fantastic. Larsen did not seem particularly curious, but he was intelligent and must have understood that Clara needed him. He should have agreed. You might think he refused in order to avoid tiresome complications; but I suspect it was to avoid one single complication – going to a place like the Armenonville, which intimidated him because he had never been there and because it was famous. To some people this cowardice will be incomprehensible, but no one should have any doubts about Larsen's friendship for Clara and for Gauna. There are feelings that do not need acts to confirm them, and friendship is one.

When she realized it was pointless to insist, Clara left Larsen to his medicines and inhalations, looked for an old notebook (which she had found at the bottom of the trunk three days before) and rang El Rubio. I think that for this particular mission, El Rubio was her 'favourite', as they say in horse-racing jargon. Out of a feeling of loyalty towards Gauna, she had tried to get Larsen to go with her, but he had one drawback: although Gauna would undoubtedly have drunk a great deal, if she was with Larsen he would have recognized her. It was with El Rubio however, that he had seen her in her mysterious disguise in 1927, and when he saw them together again he would think only of that unknown girl in the mask. Clara had no reason to suspect that Gauna had ever recognized her as that masked girl.

LI

She had to argue a long time before the boy agreed not to fetch her before eleven and then to take her straight to the Armenonville. However, he should not be judged too severely. It was Clara who had rung him, and plenty of people (including ourselves) would have made the same mistake – of thinking it was for another reason. In the shady, tree-lined calle de Belgrano the boy stopped the car, complimented Clara on her beauty and her domino costume, and made one last attempt. Finally he understood that her refusal was genuine, and tried not to seem disappointed. They spoke of mutual friends, of Julito, Enrique and Charlie.

'Have you seen them recently?' asked El Rubio.

'Not since 1927. You know what?'

'No.'

'I've got married.'

'How's it going?'

'Very well. And what are you up to?'

'Not much,' replied the boy. 'I'm studying law, not through choice. And I spend all my time dreaming. Can you guess what of?'

'No.'

'Of women and cars. For instance, I'm walking down the street and I think: I must cross to the opposite pavement – that girl just ahead looks very pretty. Or else I dream about cars. To be honest, I dream about this car I've bought myself. Haven't you noticed that Julito no longer drives me around in his Lincoln? I've just bought this car.'

It was a green car. Clara praised it and tried to look at it with interest.

'Yes, it's not bad,' continued the boy. 'An Auburn, 8-cylinder, 115 horsepower, amazing speed. Am I boring you? I'm such a bore on the subject that my friends drew lots, and it fell to Charlie to beg me, on behalf of them all, to stop going on about Auburns.'

Clara asked him why he wasn't studying engineering.

'You think I understand how it works? Haven't a clue. If this thing breaks down, don't count on me; we'll have to leave it in the street. I'm into the literature of cars, not the science – and I can assure you it's a very poor literature.'

They got to the Armenonville. With some difficulty the boy found a parking-place. Clara put on her mask and they went in.

LII

When they went into the Armenonville, Clara thought: 'How shall I know if he's here? How shall I find him among all these people?' The orchestra was playing *Horses*, which was already an old tune. If you hear it, you will undoubtedly find it banal and monotonous. It struck Clara as sinisterly strange; from that night on she could not hear it without shuddering. She realized she was frightened and that she would not be capable of seeing him, even if he were right in front of her. The head waiter, menu in hand, nodded to her and to the boy and they followed him between the masked dancers.

At that moment, as they followed the ceremonious man in black through the masked crowd who were dancing, shouting and blowing whistles that were insistent and expressionless – or expressive simply because of their insistence – Clara wondered whether she was entering a magic hall where the third night of the carnival of 1927 was going to repeat itself. 'Don't let me meet him,' she said to herself. 'Don't let me meet him. If I don't meet him, there won't be a repetition.' In reality, she was not afraid that there would be. It did not seem likely to her that a miracle would occur. The man in black led them up to the counter of the bar.

Frowning, as if communicating a fact of deep interest, the boy explained gravely: 'I've given a good tip. You'll see, he'll get us a table.' Clara noticed that when he spoke, the boy moved his lips a lot. Some hours later, when she was closing her eyes, lips moving with repugnant elasticity appeared before her, and also a toy she had had in her childhood: a kind of rubber ball, a very white little face. Someone had shown it to her, saying 'Agapito, stick out your tongue.' The little face, deformed by the pressure of fingers, stuck out an abnormally long red tongue. The memory of that face and of another, a large clown face with a huge open mouth, which was a skittle, given to her on her fourth birthday by an aunt, always made her feel slightly sick.

The boy led her out to dance. She kept thinking: 'It will be better if I don't meet him. If I don't meet him, there won't be a repetition.' She was thinking that when she saw him. At once she forgot everything: the boy, the dance, what she had been thinking. In ecstasy, her heart heavy with tenderness, she ran towards Gauna. Seeing him without Valerga and without the boys, she thought her precautions had been wildly excessive and that they were safe.

Later she said that she ought to have been suspicious but could not be; that she ought to have realized everything was taking place in too pleasant and effortless a way, as though under a spell. But she could not understand it then, or if she understood it, she could not free herself from its influence. In this lies the secret horror of enchantment: the spell. She was drugged by it, she was wrapped up in it. Clara tried to resist until in the end she abandoned herself to what presented itself to her as happiness. At a certain moment, brief but very intense, she was so happy that she forgot all prudence. And that was enough for destiny to be unleashed.

Without anyone giving an order, a waiter brought them champagne. They drank, gazing into each other's eyes. In a deliberate and solemn tone, Emilio said:

'Perhaps I imagined two loves. Now I see that there was only one in my life.'

She understood that he had recognized her. She stretched out her arms, took him by the hands, leant over the tablecloth and sobbed with gratitude. She was on the point of removing her mask but she remembered the tears and thought she had better look in the mirror first. He led her out to dance. In Gauna's arms she felt even happier and utterly safe. Then there was a strident clash of cymbals, the music changed, got quicker and more agitated and all the dancers, as though driven by a devilish glee, joined hands and ran snake-like, in a long line. There was another clash of cymbals and Clara found herself in the arms of a masked man and saw Gauna with another girl. She tried to extricate herself; the masked man held her firmly and, looking behind him, gave a theatrical roar of laughter. Clara saw that Gauna was looking at her anxiously and smiling at her with sad resignation. The dance separated them. Oh, it separated them fearfully.

'Allow me to proceed to introductions, my dear lady,' declared the masked man, continuing to dance the Charleston all the while. 'I'm a writer, a poet, a journalist perhaps, from one of the twenty or so sister republics. Do you know how many there are?'

'No, I don't,' said Clara.

'Neither do I. It's enough to know that they're sisters, isn't it? And what sisters! A resplendent necklace of girls, each younger and more beautiful than the one before. But the most beautiful is undoubtedly the one whose face is Buenos Aires, your native land, my dear. You're not going to tell me you're not Argentine?'

'No, no, I am.'

'I'd already guessed it. Buenos Aires, what a grand capital. I arrived yesterday and I still haven't seen the whole of the city. It is the Paris of America, don't you think?'

'I don't know Paris.'

'Who can say they do know it? I studied there in the Cité Universitaire for nearly three years, and do you think I dare to say I know it? Not at all. There are those who maintain that only in Italy can one make discoveries; according to them the beauty of Paris is too calculated and formal. Well, I've got my reply to those people. I discovered something in Paris. It was on a Saturday night, towards the end of winter, when I was coming back after having had dinner with a group of friends, all very agreeable people, at about three in the morning. Not at three – at twenty past three to be precise. I discovered the Concorde. What do you think of the Concorde?'

'Nothing. I don't know it.'

'You must get to know it, as soon as possible. Well, I discovered the Concorde that night. There it was, all lit up, the fountains playing and no one except me to see it. There was the banquet: the sandwiches and cakes on the table, the champagne flowing, the candles in the silver chandelier, the lace table-cloths, the lackeys in bronze livery, everything prepared, everything prepared for absent guests. If I hadn't passed by, the banquet would have been wasted.'

As the orchestra finished playing, the man, like a skilled artist, finished his speech; but at this satisfying moment his very desire for perfection betrayed him: he spread his arms out to make the ending even more poetic, and Clara fled into the crowd.

LIII

She ran towards where she thought Gauna's table was, but she could not find it. She looked for it hurriedly, afraid the masked man was following. When she saw the orchestra at the other end she felt disoriented. Then she stopped to think: they were playing a tango, so it couldn't be the same orchestra. The jazz band was at one end of the hall, the Argentine band at the other. Suddenly Clara felt almost dizzy and very confused. The two glasses of champagne she had drunk with Emilio could have been responsible for the sense of well-being she had felt a short while ago, and perhaps also for the moment of abandon and of safety; but not for this anguish. She was clearly terrified. If all was not to be lost, she must get herself under control.

Clara made her way to the bar.

As in a delirium, she watched herself walking among grotesque masks. I do not think this vision of herself was due to feminine vanity; nor do I think that it was a case of thinking only of oneself when caught in a terrible situation, like so many women – or perhaps one should say so many people. She saw herself from outside because in a sense she was outside herself. It seemed to her that she was guided not by her own free-will but by another and greater power, controlling events in that hall from above. Gauna, Valerga, the boys, El Rubio, the masked man and all the rest had lost their wills. No one noticed it except her: that was why she saw everything, including herself, from outside. But Clara told herself that this was a delusion: she was not outside. Like the others, she was in the power of destiny.

In accordance with what had been foreseen, destiny had taken charge of the situation. While she was thinking about this, she had an intuition that it was wrong, that the world is perhaps not so strange, or rather that it is strange in its own way, accidental or circumstantial, but never supernatural.

She looked in the direction of Gauna's table, which she thought she knew. She did not recognize the people sitting there. Suddenly, jubilantly, she saw Gauna among them; and suddenly, with horror, she recognized Valerga and the boys. All this happened in the space of a few seconds.

El Rubio appeared at her side at the bar. He was very happy; he was smiling with his elastic lips and talking. 'What does this devil want,' she thought. Half-surprised and half-disgusted, she heard him as if he were very far off, in another world, and his stupid desire to intrude on her were reaching her from there. What was this devil talking about? About his joy at having found her. And hesitantly, awkwardly, he was asking whether she had believed all the bad things he had said about himself. He said it with such modesty that she smiled at him out of compassion.

When she turned her head she realized that Gauna had seen her smile. Now he was looking at her with a gloomy expression. His feeling seemed to be not so much annoyance as despair and sadness.

LIV

Bewildered and deeply disturbed, Clara followed Gauna's movements. Motionless, paralysed by the fear of finding that everything that had been predicted on that rainy afternoon was actually happening, by magic, she watched Gauna speak briefly to Valerga, get up, put some money on the table and slowly move off with his friends.

The band had stopped playing. People were going back to their seats. There was a strange moment of silence and calm (in contrast, no doubt, to the hubbub that had prevailed before). It was then that Clara knew that her terrible premonition was being confirmed. Since a certain moment, impossible to pinpoint exactly, the present time had merged into the carnival of 1927. Clara ran after Gauna; El Rubio came up to her and took her by the arm, but she managed to shake him off. Crossing the hall, once again crowded with dancers, was slow and laborious. At last she got to the door and ran outside. There was no sign of Gauna or the others. She went in again and found the doorman, a very tall man in a long red coat with brass buttons. He had a small head, an aquiline nose, with small half-closed eyes and an ironic expression. She asked him:

'Did you see some men go out?'

'A lot of people have gone out and come in,' the doorman replied.

'There were five of them,' explained the girl, trying to hold back her impatience, 'an older man and four young men. They weren't in fancy dress.'

'They should have been,' said the doorman. 'Everyone

here is in fancy dress.'

Clara made her way to the cloakroom, which was looked after by the two Spaniards. (She was aware that El Rubio was following her timidly.) One of them said he thought he had seen them, but the other said he hadn't.

'Just now? Five of them, not in fancy dress? Not even in masks? Not even false noses? No, miss. I'd certainly have remembered them.'

Clara glanced again at the other one, but he just shrugged his shoulders and shook his head ambiguously.

She turned towards the boy.

'Would you like to do me a favour?' she asked.

'Anything you want.'

She took him by the hand and hurried outside with him. She said: 'I want you to drive me somewhere.'

'Wait a moment,' he said. 'I must look for my hat.'

Clara held on to him. 'You can look for it afterwards,' she murmured. 'There's no time now. Run.'

They rushed to the car. They felt they were being pursued; the pursuer managed to throw something in the car through the side-window. It was the boy's hat.

By a spectacular bit of manoeuvring and a loud squeaking of tyres, the boy accelerated and speeded down the Centenario, proud, perhaps, of his Auburn. She directed him first to the lakes and then towards the wood. They drove slowly along the narrow tracks through the wood. Clara asked him to switch on his head-lights and shine them among the trees. She was in anguish.

'What's the matter?' asked the boy.

'Nothing.'

'What do you mean, nothing? You're treating me very badly,' the boy complained. 'All day long you've been making use of me, and you won't tell me why. If I knew, maybe I could help you. Why don't you explain?'

'There's no time,' Clara declared.

But he insisted.

'You won't believe me,' Clara told him. 'Not that it matters whether you do or not. But it's true and it's horrible. And if we waste time now we shall never be able to stop it.'

'Won't be able to stop what? And do you think we're going to find anyone like this, just with a head-light? We'll need more than luck to do that. Who are you looking for?'

'My husband. He was at the dance. He saw us.'

'He'll get over it,' the boy assured her.

'No, it's not that. You don't understand. He went out with some boys, friends of his. At least, he thinks they're his friends. But they are going to kill him.'

'Why?' asked the boy.

They shone the head-lights under the railway bridges.

Clara countered with another question: 'Do you remember the 1927 carnival?'

'Yes, I remember it,' said the boy. 'I remember how you were interested in some boy, and I helped you to get him out of the Armenonville.'

'That boy is now my husband,' said Clara. 'He's called Emilio Gauna. I met him that night.'

'Yes, you asked me to help you get him out. I didn't want to bother about him, but you were so worried that I couldn't say no.'

It had been hard work getting Gauna out, that night in 1927. He had had a great deal to drink. El Rubio had given him another drink. 'I don't understand this,' he admitted, 'because I don't drink myself, but it may work.' It did. They had got Gauna out without difficulty and put him in a taxi. 'Where shall we send him?' asked El Rubio. Clara had not wanted to leave him. The three of them had driven round and round Palermo. In the end El Rubio had remembered Santiago and El Mudo, caretakers of the KDT Club, who now lived in a little house on the landing-stage by the lake, and after much pleading he had got Clara to agree that they should leave the drunken boy there. El Mudo had looked after him because Santiago was away that night. They left Gauna sleeping in a camp-bed, wrapped in a grey blanket. As a reward Clara had allowed El Rubio to take her home. He had tried to re-assure her by saying: 'Your friend is in good hands. Excellent people. I've known them all my life. They've been caretakers at the Club ever since the old days when Rossi

207

was manager, and they carried on with Kramer afterwards, till the end. I can remember how excited they used to get when we played against the fifth division of Urquiza or Palermo Sportivo. But we always used to lose.'

These reflections, or perhaps the fact that by recalling them he was recalling his childhood, moved him at first, but suddenly they made him see how the girl had played with him not just once but twice. Twice she had led him on, raising his hopes, only to make use of him unscrupulously in her intrigues with another man. He got very annoyed and stopped the car abruptly.

'Do you know something, my dear?' he asked in a tone of voice that she had never heard before.

He had put on the brake and switched off the engine. Leaning against the door, one hand on the wheel, his hat around his neck, he looked at her through half-closed eyes, with an expression that was both grim and contemptuous.

'Do you know something? Can't guess? Well, I'm fed up, fed up with this job.'

'What job?' asked Clara.

'Of serving you and your crazy whims.'

'Please, in the name of all you hold sacred, *please* go on searching. They are going to kill Emilio.'

'Going to kill him! He must be driving you round the bend. That was what you thought last time.'

The boy tried to take her in his arms and kiss her.

'No, stop. Calm down,' Clara begged him. 'Calm down and listen to me. They *were* going to kill him that time too.'

'How do you know?'

'I'll explain it to you. I didn't know him then. I met him that night, at the dance. And suddenly I knew that I had to get him out of there, because those men were going to kill him.'

'Pure intuition, eh?'

'I don't know, I promise you. I've never spoken to anyone else about the presentiment I had that night. I haven't even spoken to Emilio or to my father. Before he died, my father entrusted me with the task of looking after Emilio. My father said to me...'

At that moment, as if without feeling and without scruple, Clara began lying, quite blatantly. Involving her dead father in the lie seemed to her a trick only the lowest would stoop to, but she did not hesitate. She realized that if she were to say: 'My father spoke to me about this on his death-bed and in a dream', her appeal would lose all its force as far as the boy was concerned. She was convinced of the appalling truth of her fears and it was vital that he should help her.

'... My father said to me: "The third night is going to repeat itself. Look after Emilio." '

Although it was in a dream that he had communicated this, Clara did not feel that essentially she had lied and so there was no change in her voice as she went on talking.

'Emilio was to die in the carnival. I now understand everything. Without my knowing it, my father sent me to look for him the time before in order that I should interrupt his destiny. I must see to it that it doesn't resume its course. It may already be too late.'

The boy's reaction was to ask her: 'How can you believe it?'

'Don't you believe it?' she replied. 'Do you know what Emilio said to me not long ago? That that night in '27 he went off with his friends.'

'The state he was in, he could have imagined anything.'

'No, please listen. He told me that he had been alone at the table, that he had seen me at the bar, and that I had smiled at you. That made him furious, and he went off with his friends. Well, that didn't happen the time before, you see. None of that happened the time before. It happened today, everything, just as he told me. Emilio had the vision because the events were in his destiny. He saw what should have happened the time before and what is happening now. And he also told me that after that he had got into a quarrel over money with one of them, a thug called Valerga, and had a knife-fight with him in the wood. If we don't stop it, Valerga will kill him!'

'You haven't got much faith in your Emilio.'

'You don't know Valerga.'

'All right. Let's go on searching,' the boy said.

They explored up and down the wood with the headlights. After a while they came to the house on the landing-stage, and the boy asked Santiago and El Mudo whether they would help search too.

LV

And meanwhile, what was happening to Emilio Gauna?

In a clearing in the wood, surrounded by the boys, as though encircled by hostile dogs, face to face with Valerga's knife, he was happy. He had never imagined that his soul was so big, nor that the world could contain so much courage. The moon was shining between the trees and he could see its reflection on the blade of his little knife and he could see the hand that grasped it without trembling. Don Serafín Taboada had once told him that courage was not everything; Don Serafín Taboada knew a lot and he knew very little, but he knew that it is a great misfortune to suspect that one is a coward. And now he knew that he was brave. He also knew he had never been mistaken about Valerga: he was indeed brave in combat. It was going to be hard to beat him in a knife-fight. It did not matter why they were fighting. Did they think he had won more money on the races and did they want to get it from him? The motive was only a pretext; it was unimportant. He had a vague feeling that he had been in that place before, at that time, in that clearing, among those trees that loomed so large in the dark, that he had lived that moment before.

He knew, or simply felt, that he was resuming his destiny again and that his destiny was being fulfilled. And that also seemed right.

He not only saw his courage, which was reflected with the moon on the calm blade; he saw the great ending, the magnificent death. Gauna had already glimpsed the other

211

side in 1927. He remembered it like a fantasy: that is the only way one can remember one's own death. He found he was once again in the dream of the heroes, the dream he had begun the night before, in the yard of the lame Araujo. He realized for whom the long red carpet had been rolled out and he advanced resolutely.

Faithless, as is the way of men, he had no thought for Clara, his beloved, before dying.

El Mudo found the body.